Beyond the Black Stump

A collection of short stories, essays, and poems

Linda Noble

iUniverse, Inc.
New York Bloomington

Beyond the Black Stump
A collection of short stories, essays, and poems

iUniverse books may be ordered through booksellers or by contacting:

iUniverse
1663 Liberty Drive
Bloomington, IN 47403
www.iuniverse.com
1-800-Authors (1-800-288-4677)

ISBN: 978-1-4401-7961-7 (sc)
ISBN: 978-1-4401-7960-0 (ebk)

Printed in the United States of America

iUniverse rev. date: 12/2/2009

INTRODUCTION

"Beyond The Black Stump"

Being brought up in Australia, I found that the expressions "Beyond the black stump" or "The other side of the black stump" were often used to denote something a long way away. Wikipedia states that "The Australian expression **'black stump'** is the name for an imaginary point beyond which the country is considered remote or uncivilised, an abstract marker of the limits of established settlement." One school of thought regarding the origin of 'black stump' is that blackened tree-stumps were used as markers when giving directions to travellers unfamiliar with the terrain.

Whatever the origin, *Beyond the Black Stump*, when my husband suggested it as a title for this anthology, took immediate hold in my mind and seemed the perfect phrase to describe this collection of diverse stories, essays, and poems.

Some of the pieces are about Australia, some are set in America, some in Southeast Asia--and you can't get much further beyond the black stump than that. They also differ in subject matter, from the fantasy of *Lucille Doesn't Live Here Anymore* to the down-to-earth *A Rite of Passage*. Many of these short stories/essays are based in fact. Some are complete fabrication - for example, my one and only foray into crime fiction, *A Girl's Worst Friend*.

I even included a couple of poems, although poetry is not something I usually write. My favorite poet is Ogden Nash, to give you an idea of my poetic taste. The two poems I have included in this collection are not comical like Mr. Nash's - just observations that came to me in rhyme.

I hope you enjoy these slice o' life offerings as much as I enjoyed writing them.

A RITE OF PASSAGE

by Linda Noble

My family lived in New South Wales, Australia when I was a kid. Some of the most expensive horseflesh in Australia was nestled in the comfy stalls of Lancelot Stud, in an area that was considered "out in the bush." My mother worked as the cook for a wealthy landowner and my father was a gardener and general helper during busy times. Pat, my 17-year old sister, finished school when she was sixteen and worked as the housemaid. I went to primary school and made a general nuisance of myself.

Being an excellent cook, Mum was never short of a job. She'd had quite a string of them - both out in the country and in the city. She'd even worked for a famous politician at one time. Every once in a while, though, she'd get tired of cooking for the city folks who tried to outdo each other with parties that cost more than my mother and father together made in a year. That's when she would hanker for a country job.

Whenever she'd start thinking about the simple country life, she'd go down to Whitcomb's, a well-known employment agency for country workers in Sydney. Whitcomb's handled everyone from domestic help to drovers and jackeroos, the Ozzie equivalent of cowboys. The office staff was always happy to see Mum because of the good reports they received from the employers they matched her up with.

Mum was not the settling kind and enjoyed the variety of jobs she tried. The fact that she didn't stay anywhere too long didn't seem to bother anybody. Luckily, my father was always ready to take off on another adventure. Even though his training was on the huge circular combs used in the wool trade, he longed for wide-open spaces and was always happiest when Mum took a job in the country.

Of all Mum's jobs, this was the best she'd had. I don't know how much she was paid, but whatever it was, it was pure gravy. The fringe benefits alone would have been enough for most people. We had a lovely, furnished, three-bedroom, brick house on the property, with our own garden: trees and shrubs and all manner of wildlife. It was an "all-found" position, which meant everything was free: housing, food, utilities, and medical care. The absolute best fringe benefit from my point of view was that I had my own horse. It wasn't one of the studs, of course; just an old nag that nobody wanted to put down. But she was mine and I called her 'Twinkletoes.'

She was quite elderly and had gray hairs in her muzzle, although the rest of her coat had stayed remarkably colorful. She was chestnut, with a white blaze on her long nose and I groomed her regularly with the oval-shaped horse brushes from the stables.

Dad said I was careless with Twinkletoes, but I loved her dearly. Maybe I didn't always close the gate when I put her in the paddock, but the gates were enormous, and hard to close without help. And she never went far when she wandered off. But even Dad admitted I was good about grooming her. It was while brushing Twinkletoes' dusty hide that I encountered some of the local wildlife.

A large driveway circled around in front of the owners' house, with a garden in the center. The little garden was surrounded by a rock wall about two feet high - just the right height for sitting on. This is where I groomed my horse. I stood on the wall to reach the higher parts of her back and neck, then I'd brush her till my arms ached. Twinkletoes loved every minute of it. She'd stand there in the hot sun, twitching her tail at the flies and closing her eyes in pure ecstasy as I'd bring her coat back to a glossy, though faded red.

One day she started to fidget as I was brushing her. Her wide-open eyes showed a lot of white around the edges and she kept shuffling her feet. Suddenly she reared on her hind legs - something she had never done before. I jumped back in surprise. I was standing on the rock wall that surrounded the garden where frangipani bushes and Banksia plants were growing. Level with where I had been standing on the wall was a blue-tongued lizard poised in the garden, ready to do his bicycle-like run.

His bright blue tongue flicked in and out and his whole body quivered. Grabbing Twinkletoes' reins, I ran to get my father, where he was turning over the dirt, ready to plant some new shrubs near the swimming pool. By the time we got back to the wall, of course, the lizard had disappeared. From that time on, though, I brushed Twinkletoes somewhere else - where there were no bushes right beside me that lizards, or other critters, like funnel-web spiders for instance, could hide. Although blue-tongued lizards are not poisonous, they're as ugly as homemade sin. There are, however, many creatures in Australia that are deadly. I didn't really understand about death, but my mother's paranoia about poisonous things had rubbed off on me.

I suppose my parents protected me too much. These days kids know about death by the time they're eight. It never occurred to me that the reason Mum was so adamant about staying away from dangerous creatures was because they could kill me. If I thought about it at all, I thought they might bite me, and it would hurt.

The family who owned the property where we lived was Joseph and Rebecca Silverman, and their two younger children, 15-year old David and 22-year old Elizabeth, along with Mrs. Silverman's mother, Mrs. Jacobs.

Mrs. Jacobs was a sweet old lady who had taken an interest in me as soon as we'd arrived at this job about a year before. She told me stories and sang snatches of songs to me. I didn't understand most of the words - I realize now she had been singing in Yiddish - but I loved hearing her songs and stories. She'd sit out on the verandah in the shade, with a tall glass of lemonade resting on the table beside her. She wore loose, flowing dresses made of light, filmy fabrics, and always had a wide-brimmed floppy hat on, with flowers or a feather stuck in the hatband.

Since my friends in the area lived a long way away, I spent quite a bit of time with Mrs. Jacobs. Her other grandchildren and great-grandchildren lived in Sydney and David and Elizabeth were both off at school, and I think she enjoyed the awe of an eight-year old when she told her stories of gypsies and magic. There were some stories that made her cry - those about members of her family who had died in what she called *konzentrationslager* in a far-off place called Germany. But even then, the word 'died' meant very little to me.

Mrs. Jacobs's daughter, Rebecca was completely different from her mother. She wore baggy old trousers, her hair was cut short, and she laughed like a man. I'll never forget one day when we went shopping in the nearest town, Murrundi, which was 30 miles away on rough dirt roads. Mrs. Silverman came striding out of the grocery store, her arms full of bags, with Mum and I staggering behind her, also with full arms. Mrs. Silverman stopped suddenly in the middle of the wooden verandah, almost causing a three-person collision, and yelled at the top of her voice, "Ben, you old bastard! How the hell are you?"

My mother stared with wide eyes as Mrs. Silverman proceeded to put the bags on the edge of the dirt road and sit on the verandah steps with an old fellow who was very obviously potted. We could smell the alcohol on him, but Mrs. Silverman didn't seem to mind. She sat with her arm around him and we even saw her taking a drink from his bottle.

Afterwards, on the way home, Mum ventured to say to her boss that the police should put someone that drunk in a cell. Mrs. Silverman shook her head sadly. "Poor old bugger!" she said. "He's really down on his luck. I dunno how much of that plonk he goes through in a day, but I took a good healthy swig, so it would be all the less that he'd drink. He's gonna kill himself with that stuff," she sighed. "We've been friends for years, Dearie, long before he lorst all his money. There but for the grace of God...." her voice trailed off.

Mum was less sympathetic than Mrs. Silverman when it came to drunks, and said: "Well, no wonder he lost all his money - he obviously drank it away."

"Oh, no, Dearie!" Mrs. Silverman said quickly. "Quite the other way around. He didn't even drink before he lorst everything. Strict teetotaler, Ben was. Y'see, what happened was, Ben's wife Lily met another bloke; Billy they called 'im. One a' the jackeroos on Ben's station out there at 15-mile Road, you know?" Mum nodded, interested, in spite of herself.

"Well, this bloke was real bloody clever. He worked his way up from being a jackeroo to being the station manager. Ben trusted him like a brother. He trusted Lily too. That was his big mistake." She laughed raucously.

"The two a' them buggers ran orf together – taking all Ben's money with 'em! Cleaned out the bank accounts, took everything out of the safe deposit box and just cleared orf. Can you believe it, Ena?" She laughed again. "Billy an' Lily -- sounds bloody silly when you say 'em together, doesn't it – anyway, they bugger orf, leaving Ben stoney broke! An' he 'adn't suspected a thing." She shook her head again.

Mum looked disapproving and Mrs. Silverman glanced at her. "What? You don't think that's enough reason for a man to start getting pickled every day, eh?" Mum nodded.

"Well, love, you know what they say: don't judge a man till you've walked a mile in 'is shoes. Poor old Ben was devastated. The wife he loved, the friend he'd trusted, and the money he'd made through his hard work - all gorn. An' if the truth be known, I swear he misses his friend more than his wife or the money.

"Ben and Bill were always together. They'd ride 'round the fences, checking for places that needed repairs, and they'd get down in the sheds with the shearers when they came around and have races between themselves to see who could shear faster.

"The two a them'd go into town on business an' end up at the pub, havin' a coupla beers - well, a coupla beers for Billy an' a coupla lemon squashes for Ben. Funny that, seeing how he is now....

"So, there's poor old Ben all alone - no money, no wife, no friend. Well, I'll tell you, Ena, you shoulda seen those vultures come callin.' Soon's they knew Ben was broke, the bank manager and the insurance codgers, and the bloke that owned the feed store, and Gawd knows who else - all come up to Ben's place wanting their money.

"Well o' course he couldn't pay. Didn't matter a damn to them that Ben's life savings'd gorn down the drain. Too bloody bad, mate, they said, and then they auctioned orf all his property and sheep, and kicked Ben out on his ear. That's when Ben started drinking. Whatever money he could scrounge from picking up bits and pieces and selling them, he spent on booze. I don't think he's been sober since." Mrs. Silverman finished quietly.

There didn't seem to be much to say after that. Mum sat for the rest of the trip in silence, thinking over what Mrs. Silverman had said, and

Mrs. Silverman seemed lost in her own thoughts. Personally, I was in awe of this woman who could sit in the street with an old drunk and live to tell the tale. But Ben's sad story was soon to take a back seat to other shocking happenings.

If Mrs. Jacobs had to die, the way she did it was better than any other way. I guess everybody wants to die in their sleep if they can't live forever. And that's what she did. When Mum went to make breakfast in the huge, gleaming kitchen one morning soon after our trip to Murrundi, the family was all in a flap.

Mrs. Silverman, who had always been an early riser, was in the habit of taking her mother a cup of tea first thing in the morning, with a couple of her favorite cream biscuits to hold her over till breakfast. After a few minutes' chat, Mrs. Silverman would then go and do her most favorite thing in the world - ride her horses.

On this morning, Mrs. Silverman took her mother's early morning cuppa to her and found her still and cold. She had apparently been dead for some hours, the doctor said later, and pulled the sheet over her face sadly.

It was the first time anyone had seen Rebecca Silverman break down. I know it scared the daylights out of me when I wandered into the kitchen for breakfast and found Mrs. Silverman sitting at the breakfast table, crying her eyes out. I stopped at the door in shock. Then I started crying in empathy - I didn't even know what I was crying about.

She looked up at me, tears making her face shiny, and put her hands out to me. I moved into her arms as though it was the most natural thing in the world, and she embraced me. We cried together for a few minutes until her husband came to lead her gently to their room, leaving Mum to take me to our house, a couple of hundred yards away.

My mother tried to make me eat breakfast, but my stomach was churning and I couldn't eat a thing. When the undertaker came in the long black car I peeped through the curtains of the living room in our cottage. When they carried Mrs. Jacobs from the big house I watched with growing horror as two men maneuvered the stretcher into the converted, black-painted ambulance parked outside, leaving Mrs. Silverman sitting on the verandah crying her eyes out while her husband tried to comfort her.

Seeing the body completely covered over was the final straw for me. I ran into the little kitchen of our cottage, where Mum and Dad were sitting having a cup of tea.

"Mum, Dad," I sobbed. "Come and help Mrs. Jacobs! She's all covered up and she can't breathe under the covers." Mum and Dad looked at each other sadly and my mother pulled me onto her lap, trying to stroke the wet hair out of my eyes.

Dad leaned over to take my hand and Mum held me close. "Linda," Mum started, then looked at Dad, searching for the right words to say.

"Mrs. Jacobs is dead, love," Dad said, looking into my eyes.

"I...know...but..." I began.

Dad went on, "She doesn't need to breathe under the covers...."

"SHE DOES! She can't BREATHE!" I looked at him beseechingly. Dad persevered though.

"Linda! You've got to listen, love," Dad said firmly. "When people die they don't breathe any more," his voice went soft again.

"But...but, she'll be all right tomorrow, won't she?" I sobbed, snatching breaths between words. I think that somewhere, deep down, I must have known that she wouldn't, but as long as I didn't admit it, it wouldn't really be so.

"No, love, I'm sorry...." I could tell he was upset, too. That made everything much worse, because Dad was always calm. I felt the pressure building up in my chest again.

"But the doctor can fix her up!" I blurted out. Dad shook his head.

"There comes a time, love," he said, "when the doctor can't make people better." Then he said something that shook me to the core: "Everybody's got to die sometime, love; it was just her time."

"Not everybody!" I squeaked, my eyes widening.

"Yes, love...everybody," Dad answered.

"Not you...and...and Mum?" My fear was growing in leaps and bounds now.

"One day, love. But not for a long, long time," Mum said soothingly, holding me closer.

"But, not Pat, an'...an'...," now we came to the real reason for my despair, "not...me?" I looked at them both, one at a time, as they tried to think of some way to soften the blow.

Evidently they didn't think of one, because Mum took a deep breath and said, "Yes, Linda. Everybody will die some day. Oh, Tom!" She turned to my father, tears in her eyes. "Why do we have to tell her this now?" She sounded exasperated with Dad.

"Because, love," Dad said, folding Mum's hand and mine in between his bigger hands, "She's got to understand about death. If she doesn't understand that death is permanent, she won't have the right respect for danger, and might not be as careful as she should be." Mum nodded as she wiped away a few tears.

"I know, I know," her voice was tight, "I just don't want her to find out the bad things about life before she's experienced more of the good things," she said.

"Can't be helped, love." His voice became brusque, matter-of-fact, as he spoke to me again.

"Come on, lass. That's enough tears for one day. Ye'll have enough tears in that hanky to fill t' bathtub tonight!" And with that he stood up and took my hand firmly.

"D'ye know what I saw down in the bottom paddock yesterday?"

He had my attention, despite everything. I shook my head, waiting for him to tell me. But he waited until I looked up at him out of curiosity before he smiled, and said, "A new foal!" My intake of breath said it all.

"Oh! Dad! Can we go down and see him?"

Already some of the pain was abating. How amazing is the human spirit, that we can put to the back of our minds something so devastating. Even though it would be taken out and reexamined from time to time for the rest of my life, for that moment the tragedy faded a little.

"'Course we can, love. Let's go." Mum stood watching as Dad and I went through the gate. As we reached the tractor, something suddenly occurred to me and I turned back.

Twinkletoes was standing at the fence, swishing her tail. I ran back to the big gate, closed it firmly, then, standing on the fence I threw my arms around old Twinkletoes' neck, and hugged her fiercely. Turning back, I saw Dad watching, smiling.

When I ran back to the tractor he heaved me up into the seat, then jumped up and sat me on his lap as he started the engine. The huge machine rumbled over the uneven ground, and I snuggled next to my father, feeling safe. We turned right at the stream, heading for the bottom paddock, and ever-renewing life.

MOONLIGHT SERENADE

by Linda Noble

The first time I remember hearing "Moonlight Serenade," I was standing against the wall in Selman's Ballroom in Sydney, twisting my fingers nervously, waiting for the customers to arrive. At 15, the thought of teaching people sometimes twice my age to dance scared me half to death.

I had been taking ballroom dancing lessons since I was eleven and had been one of the students chosen to work at Selman's for the Friday Night Social. For a few shillings each, three girls and three boys from the Barrett School of Dance would join the experienced instructors who worked at Selman's full time, to help them out on their busiest night, Friday.

The male instructors, both full time and part time, would show the women customers some basic steps and the females would show the men. The goal was for the drop-in customers to become so enamored of ballroom dancing that they would sign up for private lessons with the 'real' instructors.

Mrs. Selman, the owner of the dance studio, told us that "Moonlight Serenade" was our signature tune, signaling the beginning of the Social. When it began to play we were to approach the customers and ask them if they would like to dance, and then, while dancing, evaluate their expertise. We were to be subtle, of course, but convince them that they needed private lessons. Nothing so obvious as, "Ouch! That was my foot! You could REALLY use some lessons!" Instead, we were supposed to show them a simple but elegant step; one they could master easily, to make them feel good, and then inform them that private lessons were available.

Scared or not, I was excited about being a dance instructor. I felt liberated. Able to make my own living? Without Mom and Dad? Wow! It was heady stuff. Maybe I could move out and get my own flat, and a car, and travel overseas like I'd always wanted to....

However, I discovered that if the only way I had to earn a living was by teaching dancing, I was in big trouble. In the first place, I'm not cut out to be a teacher. I'm far too impatient. The steps we were showing the customers were so simple to me--which was only natural considering all the lessons I'd had--that I found it hard to keep my impatience from showing.

Forgetting the fact that I danced six nights a week, what with my own lessons, training for competitions, and social dancing, I became unfairly annoyed with my customers when they tripped over my feet for the fifteenth time. Too young and shallow to realize that if they had any natural rhythm at all they probably wouldn't be there, I fussed and fumed inwardly when, after all my hard work, the men I was teaching would just stand there looking at their feet as though wondering where they had come from.

That wasn't the worst of it, though. Slow learners I guessed I could live with. What I remember most about my short stint as a dancing instructor was the smell. Selman's was in Sydney, Australia, and for several years there had been an influx of immigrants from Greece, Italy, and other European countries. These people were called--not unkindly, just as a way of identifying them--New Australians.

Of course their diets were much different than ours. They put tons of garlic and different herbs and spices in their food, which affected the way they smelled.

Back then, men wore suits and ties to dances, so they did a fair bit of sweating. Also, for some unknown reason, all the European men who came to Selman's seemed to have the same fetish for the aftershave lotion called, "Old Spice." The result was quite a ripe old pong floating around the ballroom.

There's something about the mixture of garlicky sweat and Old Spice that tells me those two do *not* belong together. I found myself trying to breathe through my mouth as much as possible, which caused me to talk strangely. Part of the charm of this social evening was supposed to be meeting new people and getting to know them. So the more I would try to stand as far away as possible, the more these poor, unknowing new Aussies wanted to dance closer! To this day, I can't stand the smell of Old Spice aftershave.

I think the only thing that stopped me from getting fired that night was my youth. Mrs. Selman had to talk to me twice about becoming impatient with the customers. Since this was my first night she'd been watching closely and felt that I wasn't hiding my feelings very well. The customer is *always* right, she insisted. I don't care how often you have to show them a step. I don't care if it takes all night: you will teach them that step. Now, if you'd rather not come here Friday nights, there are many other students that Mr. Barrett recommended to me... She left her sentence dangling.

I learned a valuable lesson that night. You can put up with just about anything for a few hours. I was very glad to get outside into the fresh air and blow off the smell I came to associate with Selman's.

As I caught the tram home, I thought over the evening: the smells, my scuffed shoes, and my bruised toes. But, somehow, with my hot little hand clutching my first real, earned money, it didn't seem so bad after all.

A GIRL'S WORST FRIEND

by Linda Noble

As Joe Bennett entered his front door he knew something was wrong. There was an eerie silence and a feeling of not being alone.

"Becky? Becky, honey? You here?" he called from the front hall. No answer. The hair on his arms was standing up, making Joe feel as though tiny insects were crawling up his arms. He moved cautiously down the hall toward the bedroom. Passing the living room door he looked inside. Nothing out of place. Nobody there. He called out again, just to be sure there was no one home.

"Becks? Where are you, hon?" The silence was absolute. Not even a clock ticking. When Joe reached the bedroom he looked through the open door before entering. The dresser drawers had been pulled out and the contents strewn around the room. Underwear, socks, t-shirts, were everywhere. Joe felt the adrenalin flow into his bloodstream. My God! We really have been robbed.

Angry now, he stepped into the room. That's when he saw his wife's body, face down on the bed, with an ugly bloodstain spoiling her white blouse. The breath escaped Joe's body in a rush and he started to go to her. That's when the gun butt came down on the back of his skull.

*   *   *   *

As Joe lay prone on the floor of his bedroom, before realization returned completely, his mind wandered over the events of the past week. It had started when his bookie began hounding him for the $5,000 he owed.

"Hey, Giddy!" Joe had said, in a hurt voice. "You know I'm good for it."

"Yeah, Joe," Gideon replied, "you an' every other bum who comes in here."

"Bum?! Hey, how long have we known each other, Giddy?"

"It don't matter if we was brothers, Joe - when somebody owes me five big ones, we may as well be strangers!"

"Jesus. I didn't know 5,000 was the magic number," Joe said, disgusted. "Whyn't you tell me before?"

"Because, Joe, like you, I'm a gambler, and I kept thinking you'd hit it big also. Each time you bet on the horses or the games, I was thinking your bad streak'd have to end some time. 'Course I was hopin' it'd end when you was bettin' with some other bookie!" Gideon laughed at his own joke. But it reminded Joe that he did bet with other bookies. He liked to spread his friendship around. Right now he was into Leo for around $8,000, and another $3,000 to Harry.

Harry. He only owed Harry $3,000. If he could borrow a couple grand, take it down to the casino - he could build it up into enough to pay all his debts and have some left over. Gideon was right. His bad streak had gone on long enough; he was way overdue.

However, Harry was reluctant to lend Joe the money, even though his interest rate was very attractive - to Harry, that is.

"Joe, I'd like ta help you out, but I got an inkling I'm not the only guy you owe money to. Am I right? Or am I right?" Harry put his enormous arm around Joe's shoulder in a friendly fashion. "Hey? Am I right? Joey boy?" His laugh rang out, sending shivers down Joe's spine. There was no humor in that laugh.

"Well, yeah, Harry...but..." Joe began.

"No buts, kid. You owe money all over town. Now, I know you got some collateral, otherwise I never woulda let ya get $3000 down - but that on'y goes so far. An' this here $2000 is the last I'm givin' ya. You don't pay the whole five thou back, plus innerest," Harry stopped to smile widely, "by the end of the month, you're gonna hafta produce that little gem your old lady's so attached to."

"Yeah, sure, Harry," Joe said, swallowing hard. "No problem."

So Joe had set off for the strip with 2,000 dollars and high hopes. He stayed at the Craps table betting the Don't Pass, like most of the big time gamblers. But it was one of those nights that Mr. Man-in-the-street dreams about; the shooters kept making their points. By the time Joe realized he should have been betting with the shooters instead of against them, he was out of money.

"Jesus Christ!" muttered Joe, catching sight of his hollow-eyed face in a mirror as he left the casino. He tried to brush his hair into some semblance of order with his hand, and straightened his tie and pulled his jacket straight. It didn't help much.

Standing outside the casino, Joe started thinking about that doozy of a ring his wife had inherited last year: a great big sapphire, surrounded by twelve square-cut diamonds. *That's gotta be worth fifty thou, if it's worth a penny*, he thought. Problem was - he'd tried to get Becky to hock the damned ring six months ago, when his losing streak first began. No dice. He'd promised to get it out of hock right away, but Becky had been emphatic.

"Jesus, Joey! Don't even think about it! This was my mother's ring. Whaddya mean, hock it? JEE-sus!" Becky had said incredulously. "This was the only thing my mother ever had that was worth anything. It's all I've got to remember her by. I just can't give it up. Not for a day, let alone a week."

So that had been that. Joey thought again that it was funny he'd never seen his mother-in-law with the ring. You'd think if somebody had something that beautiful they'd wear it all the time.

Time for desperate measures now, though. If Becky wouldn't let him have it willingly, he would just have to take it. If he could just find where she hid it when she wasn't wearing it, he could tell her they'd had a robbery - maybe mess up the place a bit. But how to keep her from calling the cops? They wouldn't be fooled by a fake burglary. O.K., so maybe he'd have to do a better job of making it look real. Break in, wear gloves, toss other rooms too, even though Joe knew she kept the ring somewhere in the bedroom. Yeah, he could do it. He began to make his plans. He would go inside first, make sure Becky was still at work, then go outside and put on the old work shoes he'd bought at Goodwill, and a pair of gloves.

* * * *

As Joe lay half-in and half-out of consciousness he heard a siren wailing. That made him sit up in a hurry, his memory flooding back. He was sorry he'd done that, as his head felt like it was going to spin off his shoulders.

"Becky?" he croaked. "Are you O.K.?" He opened his eyes. The spinning hadn't stopped yet and he saw multi-colored spots floating around in random patterns. He began to pull himself up slowly, using the drawer-less dresser. One look at the bed was enough to make his stomach heave. He tried to control his stomach muscles by breathing deeply through his mouth, all the time hearing the sirens coming closer.

Now he heard a screech of tires outside and feet pounding on the front porch. The doorbell rang insistently, and he could hear voices yelling, "Open up! Police!"

When nobody opened up, the door was shoved open and two police officers assumed the 'ready' stance, each holding a gun with both hands.

"In here," Joe managed, his voice a little stronger than a croak this time.

Two police officers appeared at the door briefly, then stood one on either side of the door.

"Hands above your head, sir!" the first one shouted.

"Hey, wait," Joe began.

"HANDS above your head, SIR!" the female copy repeated, even more loudly.

"But I'm the victim, here!" Joe said indignantly.

"Then you won't mind putting your hands above your head," yelled the other officer.

Joe sighed and complied. As he looked over at Becky's body lying on the bed the shock began to set in. He shook his head sadly, tears welling in his eyes. The officers came into the room, one frisked Joe expertly, the other headed for the body on the bed.

"Is she...O.K.?" Joe asked, tentatively. The male officer looked at him, calculating the chances that this man was the murderer. He looked at his female counterpart, and they both looked at Joe - not saying a word.

"I...I just came home an'...an' I found her like this. She's not *dead*, is she?" Joe's voice rose as panic took hold.

"I'm afraid so, sir. It looks like the bullet went straight through," the policewoman said. "Tell us what happened. And, Ted," she indicated the phone on the bedside table, "Why don't you call the medics."

Joe's legs suddenly felt weak and he half-fell, half-sat in the chair next to the dresser.

*　　*　　*　　*

The next few days were the worst in Joe's life. Grief mixed with worry about his own future made him very depressed. He was placed under house arrest. He had given his statement, several times, to a lieutenant down at the station, and spent most of the day wandering from room to room, wondering what to do with himself. He wasn't to leave town. He wasn't to go anywhere without telling the police where he was going. At least they hadn't put him in jail, he thought thankfully. But why all these questions they'd asked about a jeweler? Did he know Roger Harper? Had he ever been in Heinman's Jewelry Store? Did his wife ever go to a bar called Smitty's? He'd tried to find out why they were asking, but the lieutenant remained close-mouthed about it.

Joe had a lot of time to think during this period, and finally he began putting things together. Had Becky been having an affair? He'd been out a lot lately. Maybe she'd picked up with some other guy. The jeweler? The ring! No wonder he'd never seen Becky's mother wearing that ring. She hadn't left it to Becky at all. The jeweler had given it to Becky! Jesus. He'd been had.

*　　*　　*　　*

Roger Harper's time didn't go much better than Joe's. How they'd got a handle on him he didn't know - maybe Smitty's wasn't as anonymous as he'd thought.

It began early one morning with a loud knock on his front door. Seven a.m.! Who the hell would come calling at 7 a.m.? He had no premonition of trouble as he shrugged into his robe heading for the door. His mind went completely blank when the two officers at the door introduced themselves. Police? After establishing that he was who they were looking for, the policewoman said,

"Mr. Harper, we need to ask you some questions about Mrs. Rebecca Bennett."

Becky? Roger felt a chill run through him. They've found out about us! Wait a minute, his mind insisted. Cops don't come banging on people's doors at 7 a.m. to check on errant wives.

"What about her?" he asked.

"Where were you last night between 10 p.m. and midnight?"

"Home, watching TV," he answered, his bones beginning to feel like jelly. "Why? What happened?"

"I'm afraid Mrs. Bennett has been murdered, sir,"

His face changed color rapidly and the policeman suggested he sit down. Roger headed for the sofa and sat heavily.

"How?" he asked nervously.

"We're not at liberty to answer specific questions, Mr. Harper. Can anyone substantiate your statement that you were here last night?" asked the policewoman.

"Ah...yeah, my mother lives here with me. We watched TV till about midnight then we both turned in." Roger was shaken by the news that Becky was dead. He suddenly felt like crying.

Just then Roger's mother came downstairs, peering uncertainly at the visitors, as though she were nearsighted and hadn't put on her glasses yet.

"Roger?" she said, "What's going on?" She glanced at the police.

"Ma'am, we're from the LVPD. We're here to ask you some questions about a murder. Can you tell me what you did last night?"

"Me! I didn't murder anybody! What do you mean, coming in here at this hour of the morning, accusing me of murder?" she replied.

"No, Ma'am, we're not accusing anybody of murder at the moment. We have to ask questions of anybody who knew the victim, so we can eliminate people."

"Who is the victim?" Mrs. Harper asked curiously.

"Mrs. Rebecca Bennett," said the officer, watching the mother's face for any sign of recognition.

"Who?" said Mrs. Harper. The officer thought that the lady was either the best actress he'd ever seen, or Mrs. Harper had never heard of Rebecca Bennett.

"Please tell us what you did last night, Ma'am," he continued, looking warningly at Roger.

"But, I never even heard of..." began Mrs. Harper.

"Yes, Ma'am. I understand. But this will go much faster if you'll just answer our questions."

Mrs. Harper looked at Roger, then at the officers, and decided to do as she was asked.

"Well, Roger and I had dinner - pork chops, salad and French bread," she answered wryly, in a tone that said, *you wanted to know*. "Then we watched TV, and went to bed," she finished.

"What time was that, Ma'am?"

"Well, let's see...we caught some of the Late Show after the news, so I suppose it was almost midnight, wasn't it, Roger?" she turned to her son. Suddenly it occurred to her that the questioning was more likely to do with Roger than herself.

"Wait a minute," she said, "Roger? Did you know this woman?"

"Ma'am," the policewoman broke in, "We'll ask the questions, O.K.?"

All four of them ended up going to the police station, with mother and son split up in the police car, the mother in the front seat and Roger in the back, each with an officer beside them. As they drove, in silence, Roger couldn't shake the idea that Becky's murder had something to do with the ring he had given her.

The ring was actually an excellent copy of one that had been displayed in Heinman's jewelry store for several months, prior to its sale. Jewelers often make copies of their more expensive pieces to keep in the show cabinet while the real pieces languish in the vault. When they have a serious buyer as opposed to the "Oh, wow, look at that!" shopper, the customer is taken to a private room, with security, to see the genuine article. After the sale of the real sapphire and diamond ring, Mr. Heinman had allowed Roger to purchase the copy at a fraction of the cost. Roger had not felt it necessary to burden Becky with all the details, and had basked in her adoration after he gave her what she thought was a very expensive ring.

*   *   *   *

The day Roger had given her the ring they'd met in Smitty's, where nobody knew who anybody else was - even if they did. 'Where the elite meet to eat' read the faded sign outside. But not many of the customers ate anything. A dingy, low-ceilinged room with a long bar down the length of one wall faced fifteen small, private booths along the opposite wall. Becky arrived first and was sipping a white wine spritzer when she spotted Roger making his way to her booth.

"Hiya, Baby..." Roger put his hand around the back of her neck and turned her face to him for a kiss. Becky ran her tongue around the inside of Roger's mouth and he responded by putting his other hand under her breast. She pulled away from him then.

"Rog-er! Don't. Somebody will see."

Roger laughed. "Don't you worry, honey. Nobody sees anything in this joint." He sat down across from her and motioned to the bartender for another for the lady and asked for a scotch and water for himself.

"Sorry I'm late, sugar. Had a little something to do first." Roger looked smug as he glanced at Becky. His put his hand in his jacket pocket and it came out holding a small, square box.

"What's that?" Becky asked, smiling, her eyes lighting up.

Roger grinned, sitting back in the seat and tilting his head to one side. "A-ha! A surprise for somebody."

Becky leaned over the table and tried to grab the box.

"Whaaat?" she drew it out, teasingly. "Am I gonna hafta fight you for it?"

Roger shook his head and grinned evilly. "Oh, no, Baby. Just the opposite. I'll show you, when we get outta here."

They stayed only long enough to finish their drinks, then headed for the door. As always in Las Vegas, they prepared themselves for going out into the blast furnace they call fresh air by taking a deep breath of the cool, air conditioned atmosphere. Once outside they made a dash through the heat to Roger's car, parked two streets away, as people in other states might make a dash through the rain.

"Where to?" Becky asked, as Roger got the car started and the air conditioning going.

"How about the <u>Sleepytime Gal</u>?" Roger looked at her, waiting for her response.

"I don't know, Rog. That's such a sleazy little motel. Why can't we go back to your place?"

"I told you, Baby, my mother lives with me. She wouldn't understand," Roger answered.

"Are you sure it's your mother? And not some other woman?" Becky asked, not for the first time.

"I told you, there's no other woman. Damn it, Becky, I can barely keep up with *you*, let alone have somebody else hanging around."

"Is that what you think I'm doing? Hanging around?" She became petulant again.

"That's not what I meant, and you know it. We could always go to your place!" he said, spitefully.

"You know damned well I'm married. I never tried to hide anything from you!" Becky retorted.

"I know, I know. I'm sorry. It just upsets me sometimes, that you're with another guy." He glanced at her. As usual Becky seemed to like the idea of Roger being jealous of Joe. She softened - again.

"I know, sweetheart. But it's not for long. I told you - we might as well be divorced for all we see of each other. I never let him touch me, you know that. And we'll be divorced soon...."

Roger turned into the driveway of the motel, where the neon light flashed constantly on and off, outlining a well built female, larger than life, long neon hair flowing, laying back in a seductive pose, hand behind her head.

Inside the room, Becky threw her purse on the table and turned to look at the scene of their adultery. There were burn marks all over the desk and the nightstands. The bathroom had thin towels hanging on the racks, and a faucet that dripped. The rust stain in the toilet clashed with the ugly green of the paint on the walls.

She looked at Roger hesitantly. That was when he pulled open the closet door with a theatrical "Ta-da!" exposing a silver champagne bucket containing ice, a bottle of champagne, and two glasses. He had obviously stopped by earlier to stash them there.

Becky smiled then and relaxed a little as Roger put his arms around her and held her close, swaying side to side, nuzzling her neck while slipping the thin straps of her dress down over her creamy shoulders.

It wasn't until after they had made love that Becky asked Roger about the intriguing little box he had in his pocket. He retrieved his jacket from the floor and handed her the box almost shyly.

"This is how much I love you," he said softly.

Becky opened the box, drew in her breath, and looked up at Roger wordlessly, her eyes shining. Then she threw her arms around his neck and let out the breath she had been holding.

"Oh, Rog!" was all she could manage.

Roger felt a slight stab of guilt as Becky stared, mesmerized, at the ring, believing it was the real article.

*   *   *   *

The day after the murder, when the police had asked Joe about the old shoes and the pair of gloves left on the verandah, he had told them he'd been planning on doing some gardening. A skeptical glance at the overgrown front yard had reddened Joe's face, but he stuck to his story. However, it fell apart when that jerk Roger, who by now Joe was certain Becky had been having an affair with, spilled the beans.

Roger, filled with guilt because he was sure the murder was connected to the ring, had told the police everything. Since he had nothing to hide, except for the fact that he'd let Becky think the ring was real, he'd decided to come clean.

Now the police were even more convinced that Joe had killed his wife.

"But the cops saw me when they came in! I had an egg on the back of my head the size of a walnut." Joe protested.

"You could have done that yourself," the lieutenant replied, coolly.

"Then what did I do with whatever I hit myself with?" Joe was getting exasperated by now.

"You were alone for a few minutes before the police arrived," the lieutenant reminded him. "You could have gotten rid of it. The only reason you're not in jail right now is we haven't found the murder weapon yet. The point is: you have the best motive for murder. You needed money. We have a string of witnesses who saw you losing heavily at the casino that night. We also know that you're in debt up to your neck. You didn't know the ring was a fake. You came to steal it.

Your wife, who also didn't know it was fake, wouldn't let you do it. You had to kill her. End of story."

Joe realized that he would have to admit what he had planned. After all, a planned, unfruitful burglary was nothing compared to a murder charge. He laid it all out for the lieutenant.

"So. You planned to rob your own wife," his voice was cold. "Maybe you went in to check the place out before you 'committed' the crime and found your wife home with the ring on. That screwed up all your plans, so you begged her to let you take it. She refused. You're desperate. You kill her. Almost the same scenario I just laid out, with a little twist."

"No! Lieutenant, I'm tellin' ya, I didn't kill my wife!" Joe's panic was showing in his face and voice. "I *loved* her!"

"Yeah. Harper loved her too, I hear – several times," the lieutenant said slowly.

Joe's face and neck went red and he looked to be on the verge of attacking the lieutenant.

"You had a fight about the ring," the lieutenant continued his scenario. "It came out that it wasn't her mother's after all, like she told you. You find out about the affair. Pow! Motive number two."

"It wasn't like that," Joe was shaking visibly by now.

A hasty knock on the lieutenant's door interrupted them. The uniformed officer had a whispered conference with the lieutenant, who looked at Joe, not saying anything. When the officer finished, the lieutenant leaned back in his chair and asked Joe, "Did you ever tell anyone about your wife's ring?"

Joe blinked at the change in questions, then remembered that he *had* mentioned it to someone. He told the lieutenant the circumstances.

"O.K., Joe," said the lieutenant, "Here's the thing: We just arrested somebody for trying to hock a ring just like the one you and Roger described. The weapon he had matches exactly with the one that fired the bullet found in your wife's body. We'd like you to look at a line-up for identification purposes."

"Sure. Anything," Joe said, relief showing on his face.

Joe could tell at the first glance that he'd seen guy number three before - and where. It made his blood boil to think that Harry, on top of robbing a fellow blind with the vig he charged, hired hoods like this one to rob, and in this case kill, innocent people. How long had he been getting away with murder?

*   *   *   *

The trial was sensational. Tommy, Harry's hired gunman, gained himself some favors by ratting on his boss. Harry was found guilty of second-degree murder, and the state decided to act on the information they got from Tommy and file further charges against Harry for aggravated robbery, organizing a numbers racket, prostitution, and running drugs.

After the trial Joe decided to move away from Vegas. Maybe to a quiet little town where people didn't go in for murder, robbery, and trafficking. He'd had enough of the bright lights, the gambling. He wanted to meet a better class of people. Somewhere near a beach for a change. Maybe Atlantic City....

JUPITER

by Linda Noble

To Poppy, riding a horse like Jupiter was the most wonderful thing she could imagine. She watched her sister, Melissa, ride him around the parade ring, sitting up proudly, dressed in beautiful, cream-colored jodhpurs and matching jacket, with a pale lemon silk shirt adding just the right touch of color to her ensemble.

Melissa waved, smiling, as she galloped past and Poppy, sighing with envy and pride, waved back. She saw her brother heading her way. Probably lunch, thought Poppy, and immediately turned her attention back to Jupiter.

"Come on, Poppy. Don't give me any trouble today, O.K.?" said her brother, Michael, grinning at her and punching her playfully on the arm. Poppy continued gazing across the parade ring, where Melissa was dismounting. Jupiter tossed his head and stamped his feet, steam pouring from his nostrils, and Poppy's heart went out to him.

"Jupiter! Jupiter! Please let me ride on you. We could ride through the forests together. Over the river, where you could jump - higher, higher - all the way to the enchanted meadow!" Poppy cried in entreaty. Except it came out "Ju-der! Juder!"

"Yes, there's your favorite, Jupiter," said Michael, helping her to climb higher on the sturdy fence, and holding on to her carefully, knowing from past experience how suddenly Poppy could move at times. "Perhaps we'll go for a ride later?" he said questioningly, smiling at her. Poppy couldn't believe her ears.

"Oh, Michael! Thank you. Nothing could make me happier! I love you, Michael!" Poppy hugged her younger brother with fervor. Michael heard her grunting, her sweet head nestled into his neck, and, typically, when Poppy showed her affection for him, he felt a lump of sadness in his throat. "Come on, Sweetie," he said gently, helping her get down from the fence.

Back at the house everyone was already seated at the lunch table. Michael took Poppy to the powder room in the hall first, to wash her hands. As they sat at the round table Melissa was happily recounting the details of her ride.

"This race is in the bag!" Melissa's eyes shone as she made the announcement. "Jupiter was superb this morning!"

"Ju-der, Juder!" Poppy chanted between spoonsful of soup. Melissa grinned at her sister. "Wipe your chin, Darling," she said absently. Poppy complied, dabbing at her chin with her napkin, still chanting "Ju-der, Juder...."

"Poppy and I are going riding this afternoon. Anyone care to join us?" Michael asked the assembled diners. Mary Atkinson sat next to Poppy so that she could help cut her daughter's food. Her husband, Paul, was to her right, then Melissa and Michael, completing the family.

"Don't think so, Darling," said his mother. "I've got some work to do in the office this afternoon."

This prosperous stud farm was run entirely by the family. Mary did most of the bookkeeping. Melissa helped when she was home from college. Michael had graduated last year, with an MBA, and was happy to be back in the place he loved most in the world. Paul dealt with the daily running of the farm; scheduling stud services, overseeing the trainers for the racing section of their farm, and generally handling all the details involved with running a successful business.

Michael had taken many tasks from his father's shoulders since returning from school, but he was never happier than when he was with the horses. He had completed his degree because he knew he would need it to run the business in the future. But if it had been up to him, he would have taken the extra time required and earned his degree in veterinary science. Still, he had to admit, here he had the best of both worlds – helping to run a family business that filled his hours pleasantly, and spending time with the animals whenever he felt like it.

After lunch Poppy looked at Michael expectantly, smiling from ear to ear. He could never resist grinning back at her, in the fashion of Dobie Gillis from the old 50s TV show, when Dobie, confronted by Zelda wiggling her nose at him, would always wiggle back.

"I have a few phone calls to make before we leave, Poppy. Why don't you sit down at your desk and draw me a picture while you're waiting? Won't be long." Michael sat his sister down, handing her a red crayon and some paper, then headed into the office.

When he came out of the office, an hour later, Poppy was sitting right where he had left her, still with the red crayon in her hand, staring at the office door. When she caught sight of him, her whole face lit up. She was so beautiful when she smiled, he thought.

"We ready?" he asked, grinning at her again. "Well, lllllllet's go... Pilgrim," Mike said in a fair imitation of John Wayne, making Poppy laugh, as always.

"Go, go, GO! Ju-der!" Poppy said out loud, while her mind and heart soared. *Jupiter and I are going to fly...jumping over everything in our way. Nobody will be able to catch us...*" "Ju-der, fwy...fwy..."

Michael helped Poppy put her coat on, put on his own, and left the house, holding Poppy's hand, heading for the stables. On the short trip to the stables Poppy was jumping up and down with excitement, chattering unintelligibly. Michael watched as she ran ahead a little, then back to him, grabbing his hand and bending her body over so she could throw more weight into dragging him toward the stable faster. She was almost as tall as he, so Michael had to put quite a bit of muscle into resisting, trying to keep from losing his balance.

She went directly to the saddling enclosure, still tugging Michael by the hand. Poppy stood suddenly still as she saw Jupiter being saddled up for another trial. Her breathing slowed down and she stared at the horse in awe, whispering "Ju-der" over and over. Michael steered her toward the gentle pony the groom had saddled for her -- a lovely little mare named Hannah -- standing placidly beside Michael's larger mount, Thunder. As Michael eased her toward Hannah Poppy started to drag her feet, holding Michael's hand with her left hand, and stretching out her right hand toward Jupiter.

"Now, Poppy! You know you can't ride Jupiter. I'll take you for a nice ride around the meadow on Hannah. Come on," Michael urged her, using all of his strength to pull her toward her gentle mount.

"NO! NO! JU-DER!" Poppy screamed. Without warning, she stopped resisting Michael's pulling, causing him to sit down suddenly in the middle of the saddling enclosure, letting go of Poppy's hand in the process. Quick as a rabbit, Poppy raced over to Jupiter, grabbed his reins, heaved herself up into the saddle, and was turning him out of the enclosure before Michael had recovered himself.

"POPPY! Come back. Jupiter's too strong for you!" Michael yelled, panicking. "Please, Poppy! Come for a ride with Michael," he yelled pleadingly.

Poppy did not even acknowledge that she heard him. With a burst of speed, holding Jupiter's reins high in the air and making loud clicking noises with her tongue as she had heard other riders make, she encouraged Jupiter to jump the fence of the enclosure. The fence was not very high, and as Michael saw Jupiter's legs clear the top he realized he could not stop the huge stallion. He stood staring in dread after his sister, his mind racing.

One of the grooms had wheeled around Michael's horse, Thunder, and ran it over to him. Michael grabbed the reins quickly, throwing his right leg over Thunder even before the horse had come to a complete halt. By this time, Poppy and Jupiter were streaking across the meadow, heading for the slow moving stream that crossed the property at the bottom of a small valley.

Poppy was in heaven. Her hair was blowing in the wind, and she could feel the powerful horse moving under her. Everything looked so wonderful from up here, she thought. She felt as though she was truly flying; all sound had abated, except for the wind rushing by her ears. There was just Jupiter and Poppy, running together. She did not hear her brother racing behind her, calling her name. She sat unsteadily in the saddle, not being used to galloping. A slow trot was the fastest Poppy had ever traveled on Hannah, and even that was with Michael holding the reins and trotting alongside on his own horse.

For the first time in her life, Poppy felt free. The awkwardness she usually felt because of her misshapen body was gone. She felt as though she sat on this beautiful horse with all the grace and elegance of a princess. She wanted this feeling to go on forever.

Perhaps because Jupiter felt the lack of expertise in his rider, perhaps because Poppy's weight shifted as she tried to sit up straighter, or perhaps because a groundhog had made a new hole in the grassy paddock - whatever the reason, Jupiter's hoof twisted and he stumbled, just as he was getting ready to leap the stream.

To Michael the nightmare scene before him seemed to be taking place in slow motion. One minute Jupiter was galloping toward the stream with Poppy holding the reins, the next, Jupiter swayed to one side as he was about to jump the stream. Then Michael stared in horror as he saw Poppy slide out of the saddle and fall, hitting her head on the large rocks in the bed of the stream.

Jupiter regained his stance without the added weight and went on to finish his jump, slowing down to a trot on the other side and turning back toward the stream. Poppy lay face down in the shallow stream, not moving.

Michael was already dismounting as he pulled Thunder to a halt near the edge of the stream. He scrambled over the rocks, quickly raising Poppy's face out of the water. A great deal of blood was mixing with the water of the stream.

"Poppy! Oh my God, Poppy!" Michael said frantically. He put his hands under her head, gently, afraid to move her. As he turned her head slowly around, he saw that the life had gone out of those sweet blue eyes, and knew there was nothing that anyone could do for Poppy. Her eyes were still wide open, but her mouth was curved into a smile of utter joy.

Not Yet Spring

by Linda Noble

It's hard for me to think, right now
of blossoms on a laden bough.
The sounds and smells and sights of spring are down
   the road a piece.

The snow is falling heavily
the temperature is, too.
There's ice and slush and freezing rain
it's winter; what else is new?

January's not the month
to try to think of spring.
Of balmy breezes, sunny days,
blue skies, and birds on the wing

But wait till April comes along
- a little early still
but close enough to think about it:
a preview, if you will.

Picture this, the April buds
are wearing their spring green,
beneath the last few clumps of snow
some grass can now be seen.

The sun is shining, weakly yet,
but promising much more,
the water in the streams and creeks
is rushing with a roar.

The ice is melting fast

and there's new wildlife to be found
chipmunks and young squirrels
skitter over the ground.

The baby birds, their mouths wide open
cheep and squawk and bleat
the foals and calves and baby deer
struggle to find their feet.

The fans look forward to baseball games,
football's in the past.
Kids count the days till summer break
and will the days to go fast.

But those of us who've seen many springs
and summers, winters, falls,
are happy just to let time pass -
at times it seems to crawl.

But that's OK,
we don't fret -
Spring will come,
but it's not time yet.

THE COUNTRY LIFE

by Linda Noble

We've all heard about those cute little one-room schools where the kids were all clean-but-poor, poor-but-honorable, with a big-hearted teacher who, although overworked, still made time for all his little students - a kind word here, a bit of encouragement there... Well, I went to a one-room school that didn't even come close to being cute, and Mr. Croskey was not even remotely like our mythical good guy.

If my story happened here and now, my guess is he'd have quite a bit of explaining to do to school authorities and parents about his lack of sensitivity at best, and cruelty at worst. But back then who cared about a little backwoods (and backwards) school in Bungendore, N.S.W., Australia? Besides, in the 50s folks were still inclined to listen to a teacher rather than a kid. When I told people that I was unhappy, they thought I was just a disgruntled city kid who didn't like it 'out in the bush.'

It started out badly the very first day. I got to school early and found some of the other children inside, drawing on the blackboard with chalk. They knew there was going to be a new kid in school since, in small communities like that one there aren't many secrets.

All of them gave me the once-over and one of the boys, Peter, asked if I wanted to draw with them. Wanting to fit in, and because I loved to draw, I took some chalk and began drawing animals, my favorite subject.

After a few minutes Peter asked if I could draw people so I drew a ballerina in a tutu, my second favorite subject. Peter said, "Betcha can't draw a man from Mars!"

I said, "'Course I can!" and proceeded to draw an alien creature with one eye dangling on the end of a large antenna coming out of the middle of his forehead. I put a comical look on his face and everybody laughed. Just then we heard footsteps on the wooden verandah. The kids scrambled for their seats whispering, "Mr. Croskey's coming!" and I turned to face the door to meet my new teacher.

Mr. Croskey was a stern-looking man, about 5'7" with dark, wavy hair He walked in, looked around, saw me standing there and came toward me. He stopped before he got to me though, and stared at something a little behind me. His jaw tightened and his eyes narrowed.

"All right, you lot," he yelled, "Who the bloody hell did that?" He pointed to the board.

Several voices piped up, "The new girl, sir!"

I didn't know what they were talking about and looked at Mr. Croskey blankly. He grabbed my shoulder and propelled me to the blackboard.

"Did you do that?" his voice snapped out, as he pointed to my Martian character. Underneath, however, someone had written, "Bloody old Croskey" in large letters. I gulped air, as I tried to tell him I knew nothing about the writing.

"B-but," I began.

"Did..you..draw..it?" He shook me by the shoulder as he spat the words out.

"Well, yes, b-but, I didn't..." I began again. His eyes flashed as he bent toward me, and slapped me hard on the side of my head, making my ears ring.

"Let that be a lesson to you! Next time you feel like messing about, you'll remember a bloody good reason not to. And if you think we're going to let some nitwit from the Big Smoke come in here and make fun of us country folks, you've got another think coming, girlie. Isn't that right, children?" He turned to the class, and they answered him, as one.

"Yes, Mr. Croskey."

"Now, sit down, and hurry up about it, before I give you a bit a' bloody encouragement!" He picked up his cane from the desk and waved it above his head, making it whistle through the air.

That was enough to galvanize me into action. I bolted to the back of the room holding my ear and fighting back tears, looking for a desk as far away from this monster as possible.

"Oh, no you don't, Noble!" his voice boomed. "Sit right here in front, where I can see you." I was shaking so badly that I wobbled over to the seat he pointed out and slid between the desk and the attached chair as fast as I could, wondering who had played such a cruel trick on a newcomer.

I looked longingly out the window. Outside, the hot Australian sun beat down on the hard-baked ground. There were gum trees and a fence made of rough wooden stakes placed at regular intervals, and two layers of sturdy steel wire in between to keep the sheep out. Some sheep were grazing in the distance, in the shade of a tree. It all looked so peaceful that it was hard to believe what had happened inside the classroom.

The rest of the day went by in a blur. Nothing really sank in. I'd never been hit before and apart from the fact that it had hurt, I was mortified, my cheeks burning with humiliation.

Of course, as soon as I got home that night I told my mother and dad what had happened. At first they were skeptical because, after all, most teachers are not that mean. But when I gave them details, they became concerned.

The next day my mother talked to the overseer of the property about the teacher. Of course she didn't like the fact that I had been hit for something I didn't do, but when she also told him she thought it was wrong for a teacher to swear in front of, let alone at, kids, he laughed!

"Ena, you've got to understand, love. This is the country. Things are different down here. We don't hold with any a' those city ways. These are farm boys and girls - they're used to what you call 'rough talk.' The sheep don't seem to mind a bit!" He laughed uproariously at his own joke.

Mum went back to her main gripe, "All the same, Bill, he did hit Linda..." Mum's voice trailed off as Mr. Gates laughed again.

"Oh, Ena! She doesn't have any bruises, does she? He didn't injure her, did he? I'll bet it only hurt her pride. Gawd's truth, if we went marching down to the bloody school every time a kid got clipped 'round the ear, we'd be doing nothing else! Your Linda'll just have to learn our country ways, love, then she'll be all right."

I did learn. I learned to keep my mouth shut and my eyes open. That first day was just the beginning. Mr. Croskey seemed to delight in making me uncomfortable. He embarrassed me often, asking questions he knew I didn't understand and then laboriously explaining the answer, as if to a five-year old. Or he would hold my work up to ridicule when I made mistakes. Before I found out what was what, I felt the cane around my legs a few times. Luckily it didn't take me too long to learn that my best bet was to lay low; never speak unless spoken to, and then, with feigned respect, and never draw attention to myself.

Mr. Croskey seemed to be especially piqued by the way I spoke. He said I talked like the "bloody Queen a' Sheba." People had been complimenting my mother and father on the way I spoke for years. 'She sounds <u>so</u> grown up!' they'd say. 'What a <u>lovely</u> little voice,' they'd say. I guess my parents didn't realize that in this school it was going to be a handicap. I didn't have to be an Einstein to realize that if the way I talked bothered him, I'd be better off not talking at all, unless I had to.

Life in the country wasn't all bad though. A few months after our arrival, Norm, one of the jackeroos, brought me a 'poddy' lamb. As the jackeroos went about their daily tasks of mending fences, seeing to the animals, and any other chores that needed to be done, they sometimes came across ewes who'd had one lamb too many and didn't know what to do with it. If the fellow who found it was a good-hearted soul who remembered how much children love baby animals, he'd bring the poddy back to the station and give it to one of the children on the property. If he wasn't, lamb was probably on the menu for dinner that night instead of mutton. Norm chose to give this one to me and I was thrilled! My mother and father were happy because, although they knew it was going to be a nuisance to care for, they were glad that I had something to think about other than school.

I called him Snowy. Not very original, but then, I was only ten. Snowy seemed like a fine name for a lamb to me. I had a vague idea that he would grow up into a bigger lamb, but for the moment he fit into both my hands and was cuddly and warm, and I loved him.

At first, we had to feed him with a baby bottle. It was obvious that Snowy had been a forced orphan for several days, for he was just skin and bones. Norm showed me how to warm the milk a little, so the lamb would take it, and I laughed at the way Snowy guzzled it down. Norm said we couldn't let him have too much at first, because his stomach had to get used to food again. Eventually, though, he was on a normal feeding schedule and I fed him before and after school, as well as coming home at lunchtime (any excuse to get away from school!) to feed him again.

It was surprising how fast Snowy grew. His growth was quite noticeable to me because he was in the habit of greeting me at the garden gate by jumping up on me like a dog would. As he got bigger and heavier it became harder to hold him, and before long he was knocking me right off my feet. As I lay on the ground, flat on my back and winded, Snowy would paw me and "baa" at me to get up and go play with him. I'd bury my fingers in his by-now thick fleece, scratching deep down, which Snowy seemed to enjoy immensely. Mum said I was silly to spoil a farm animal like that, but I figured whatever treatment Snowy got from me, he deserved, because he was my savior during those miserable days at the one-room schoolhouse.

I took to telling Snowy all the hateful things that happened to me. We'd sit in the meadow after I came home from school, Snowy lying, again, like a dog, with his head in my lap, and I'd scratch underneath all his wool and talk a blue streak. I never talked at school, unless ordered to by Mr. Croskey, and the other kids were afraid to talk to me because they wanted to stay on Croskey's good side. Besides, as long as he was picking on me he left them alone. So Snowy was my only friend in good old Bungendore.

One of the worst days I had at that school was in early December. The sun was shining and all the windows were open, since it was almost summer, and we were having art class. With my determination not to let old Croskey make me cry I had developed a hardened attitude. I would sit stonily whenever he hurled insults my way, and I'd clench my mouth tight to keep from crying when he clipped me under the ear or caned my legs for minor infractions. But this day he did something unforgivable - he attacked my artistic ability! That was a different kettle of fish.

Our task was to draw our interpretation of Santa Claus. This was something I could do with gusto, since drawing was the one thing I knew I could do well. I had a brand new box of colored pencils with nice sharp points, and a huge piece of pristine white art paper. What more could a kid who likes to draw ask for?

I really got into the project, drawing a light pencil outline, then darkening it as I became more confident about its shape. Santa's fat tummy had a big, wide, black belt, and his suit was trimmed with white fur, which I made by making an outline of light strokes with the pencil, letting the white of the paper form the broad trim around the jacket and the hat. He had his arms up over one shoulder, with an enormous sack in his hands. Out of this sack poked a bit of a train, part of a game, and my pride and joy, the upper half of a doll with pigtails. I even put cute little freckles all over her face.

I colored everything carefully, not going outside the lines of course, losing myself in the project, and feeling happy for the first time in ages. As usual, my tongue was sticking out of the side of my mouth as it does when I'm thinking hard about something and I was humming a bit. That was a mistake. Rule No 1: never draw attention to yourself in the enemy camp.

I was so engrossed in my picture that I didn't see Mr. Croskey walking up and down the aisles until it was too late. He stopped at my desk, made an exaggerated gesture with his hands, throwing them up in the air and then clasping them together in front of his face.

"Oh! Children! Look what I've found! A PERfect example of Father Christmas!" He snatched my drawing out from under my nose and carried it between his finger and thumb to the front of the class. Facing us, he held the drawing up high, gripping it on each top corner.

"Can you believe it? Here it is, a perfect example..." Here he paused; the other children were staring, open-mouthed, hanging on his every word. "A perfect example," he continued, "of what not to do!" he yelled.

The children started snickering nervously. Things were normal after all. He wasn't going to praise my drawing after all, far from it.

"What did I tell you bloody kids about this project, hmmm?" The children, used to his rhetorical questions, didn't utter a word.

"Jill!" he said to one of the third class girls, "Didn't I say I wanted an *interpretation* of Father Christmas?"

"Yes, Mr. Croskey." Jill mumbled.

"Yes, Mr. Croskey! That's right, Mr. Croskey! You see? Even a little 3rd class kid understood!" he boomed.

"Neil?" He turned to another child, in 4th class, "Did I say I wanted a picture like the ones you see on the bloody Christmas cards those stupid companies sell to an even more stupid public? Hmmm?"

"No, Mr. Croskey," Neil said, smirking.

"No, Mr. Croskey is right! Full marks for Neil!" At this, Mr. Croskey took the drawing and ripped it in half, then put the pieces together and ripped them again.

"Now Miss Smartarse, would you kindly draw a picture with some depth - some personality?" He tossed the torn bits of my drawing on my desk and continued down the aisle.

"Now this," he said, picking up little Narelle's drawing, "is more like it. You see how there are no hard and fast lines? Just a bare outline with a vague shape, colored in blue instead of red? That shows character, individuality. Narelle is only in first class this year, but already she shows promise." With one last, disgusted look at me, he marched back to the front of the class and dismissed us.

Oh, Snowy got an earful that night! As I sat hugging him, my tears mingling with his oily wool, he pawed me sympathetically. At least it seemed that way to me.

But, like everything else in life, my sojourn into hell was to come to an end - and shortly.

My mother had been hired as a cook at this, the largest station in the area, mostly to provide fancy food for the parties held for the station owner's twenty-year old daughter, Jennifer. Mum had cooked for I-don't-know-how-many gala events since we'd been there, as well as preparing wonderful meals for the owner's family every day.

But the highlight was Jenny's twenty-first birthday party. People from all over the country came to the party, either staying over at the big house, or renting rooms in town. Mum worked all hours for weeks ahead of time to fashion all sorts of fantastic concoctions for the 'do.'

Even I was able to help a little. My job was to bend the warm brandy snaps around the broom handle, making a tube that my sister Pat, who had come down from Sydney to help with the party, could squeeze cream into. It was the social event of the season and Mum was praised uphill and down dale for all the wonderful food she provided.

The week after the party, my mother was told her services wouldn't be needed any more. Jenny was going to live in Melbourne with her aunt, to get ready for her wedding, which was to take place in a few months. After that the bride and groom would be living somewhere else, and her parents wouldn't need a cook just for the two of them.

So, after a year and a half of hard work on my mother's part and grief on mine, we were shunted back to Sydney on the train.

After a tearful farewell with Snowy, who by now had enormous, curled horns (he was a ram, after all), Mum, Dad and I took off in the steam train to Sydney, where we would lick our wounds for a few weeks before Mum found a new job.

Dad went back to the business he was trained for - working on the huge circular combs used in the first process of the wool trade, instead of filling in as an extra hand on the sheep station.

Snowy turned out to be a big, very woolly ram which, now that his fleece was valuable, was drafted into the same flock that had kicked him out a year earlier.

I'm sure that life in Bungendore didn't change any for us having left. Maybe Captain and Mrs. Mueller, the property owners, would have to settle for plain old mutton for dinner instead of Mum's elegant dishes, and perhaps bloody old Croskey had to find another whipping boy or girl to take out his frustration on, but other than that, life would go on as usual.

As the train pulled away from the station, heading north for Sydney, I looked out at the fields and meadows, watching kangaroos hopping off into the distance. Although it was a wonderful sight and the countryside looked like something from a postcard, I was really looking forward to getting back to the city – and a new school.

Thinking back on my days in Bungendore, I couldn't help but feel sorry for Jill and Neil, and the others, who had no choice but to stay in that little schoolhouse until they were 16 and could escape. I wouldn't have wanted to be in their shoes for all the tea in China.

SOME DAYS ARE LIKE THAT

by Linda Noble

'Oh, my God! Where *is* he?' Marge thought, looking desperately around the casino. 'I *knew* I shouldna let 'im outta my sight! He told me he'd be back in two hours *four* hours ago! Now what the hell are we gonna do? He's got all the money for rent, food, bills. He *swore* he wouldn't gamble it all - just a little, he said. An' I believed him! Je-sus!'

The casino was crowded, as usual, and the noise of the slot machines, the dealers and the people was making her head throb. Usually, Marge loved to come here. The excitement, the glitz, the fun of watching people having a good time had a tranquilizing effect on her. But tonight, what with the drop-off in Bobby's overtime, the extra medical bills for Tim, and the fact that Bobby had been a little drunk when he left to play the tables, made her very nervous.

"Hey, sweet lips!" a voice to her right said. "How's about a little peck for your old man, huh?"

"*Bobby*," she said, sagging with relief. "God, I was worried! You were gone so long! You didn't...." her voice trailed off as she looked at him apprehensively.

"Naw! I *told* you I wouldn't gamble all our money, Sugar! An' I meant it. I did have just a *little* flutter, though. An' look what I brung ya!" Bobby waved a fistful of $20 bills in front of Marge's face, with the biggest grin she'd seen on him in a very long time.

GRAM

by Linda Noble

She sits staring out of the window as the rain comes down in torrents, a slight frown making the lines on her face show up more than usual. At 90 years of age, she has good reason to be wrinkled.

Her white hair has thinned over the years, but she still has a handsome look about her. One can tell at a glance that once she was a beautiful young woman. She wears glasses, of course, but these days even they are not enough to allow her to read. She needs to use a magnifying glass, too - a big one. Her knees give out on her whenever she walks, and getting up out of a chair takes forever. When she tries to do anything with her hands, they won't cooperate. "My hands aren't my own today," she'll say with a chuckle.

In the morning, once she has maneuvered the bed and bathroom, and dressed in her flowery dress and pearls, she ambles toward the television set and turns it on. First things first: the Home Shopping Club has to be turned on. She stands there a while, watching the people she has grown to love, smiling at them and talking to them as though they could hear her.

She makes her way to the little kitchenette to heat up some water for coffee and remembers that her daughter, Martha, a 70-year-old widow, had been to visit the day before and left her some sweet rolls. She takes one and chews it slowly, while waiting for the water to boil.

Coffee made and another sweet roll in hand, she heads back to the tiny living room to talk to her friends on HSC. This occupies her time for the next two hours until gradually her head droops forward and she naps.

A bell awakens her and she tries to focus on the TV to see what the "special deal" is. She sees Holly holding up a beautiful gold ring, with large blue stones ranged in a circle with a single, large clear stone that looks like a diamond in the center. She draws in her breath, entranced by the gorgeous ring - and for only $29.95! She reaches for the phone at her side and pushes the button marked "1," activating the speed dialing system that her grandson programmed for her long ago.

After a nice chat with the girl who answered the phone (who got more than she bargained for when she said "Hel-lo! How are you?"), the ring is ordered and Gram sits back contentedly to watch the show, wondering who she can give the new ring to.

Every once in a while, she glances at the window, only to find that the rain is still falling. However, since she is cozy and warm in her little apartment and has nowhere she needs to go today, it's no great inconvenience.

Still...she does like to see that sun shining. Somehow, rain always depresses her and makes her think of things she would rather not think about - being young, dancing, laughing.

Some people enjoy their memories of long ago, but they only make Gram sad.

BYRON BAY

by Linda Noble

Byron Bay, New South Wales, Australia. Today it's a thriving resort area. When I lived there in the 1950s it was a little known, beautiful, coastal town. Nearby Ballina was well known for its whales; there were regular boat trips leaving, full of passengers pursuing the popular activity of whale watching. And Lismore was the local commerce center where people from all the smaller, local areas did their shopping. But Byron Bay remained a sleepy little town.

My sister Margaret and her husband Jim lived there, high on a hill with a terrific view of the Pacific Ocean. That real estate, today, is worth a fortune. Marg and Jim were renting a very nice old house at the time. Made of weatherboard, with a corrugated tin roof, there was lots of room for a family of five. A huge water tank sat outside the back door. This is where the snakes liked to gather.

I remember heading out for school one day, walking out of the kitchen door and almost stepping on a three-foot garter snake; harmless, but scary all the same. He was sunbathing on the wide back step. As I opened the door and put my foot on the step, he hurriedly slithered away. I yelped, startled, but not too loudly. This was pretty typical for the early spring.

I was staying there with my sister and brother-in-law and their two boys, Michael and John because Mum had taken yet another job in the country. This one, however, had stipulated no children. Dad had decided to stay at his bread-and-butter job in Sydney, waiting to see how Mum's latest venture panned out before joining her. By that time it was hoped that they could make some more permanent arrangement for me. My other sister, Pat had a job in Sydney – and anyway, she was only 19 herself and rooming with a friend. That left no one to take care of me for the moment. So there I was in a dream location, but too young to really appreciate of it.

I was disappointed when my parents wouldn't let me go away to boarding school, even though I begged them to. I'd been reading all of Enid Blyton's books, many of which dealt with boarding schools. In the Mallory Towers series the kids had such fun and everybody had lots of friends that I longed to go to one. But when Mum said no, that was it.

Since Margaret is 14 years older than I, she was more like a mother to me than a sister. Even though she was only 25 at the time, she was a born caregiver – and strict. I got in just as much trouble with her as my nephews did. I had fun with Michael (5) and John (3), though. Since I was older than they, I lorded it over the two boys. They were both little buggers, as my sister was fond of saying; always getting into trouble. But one way I could control them was when I'd stage impromptu plays in the living room. They loved to be entertained.

A blanket strung between one of the windows on the front verandah and the radio, which sat on a tall sideboard served as our curtain. I would catch the corner of the blanket in the window and shut it tight, then anchor the other end under the heavy radio, leaving the bulk of the blanket dangling to the floor. Then I'd act out bits and pieces of the latest pictures we'd been to see; singing whenever the need arose. They would sit on the couch and grin and clap at my antics.

Going to the pictures in Byron Bay in those days was a lot different than it is today. There was no real movie theater, so the screen and movie projector were set up in the local library. The best part was the chairs we sat in. They were deck chairs, like the kind you see on ocean liners, made of canvas and wood. Very comfortable! We'd sit or lie there in our chairs and watch Miss Doris Day singing her way through *Calamity Jane*, or whichever movie was showing that week.

The beach – and the Pacific Ocean – was a five-minute walk from our house. We'd often take a picnic lunch and sit, sheltered from the wind by a large sand dune, and sunbathe, while picking pigface, a fleshy plant that grows abundantly on the sand dunes in that area. We'd absently pick off the fat, triangular leaves and squish the liquid out of them as we lay prone on a towel, listening to our transistor radio.

Although most of my memories of Byron Bay are good, there's one that isn't. And I have the scar to remind me. Margaret and Jim had gone away for the weekend on the train to see some friends in another town. I didn't want to go with them because I would miss Guy Fawkes Night, otherwise known as bonfire night. So they arranged for me to stay overnight with some old friends in town.

Guy Fawkes was a Catholic rebel who planned to displace Protestant rule by blowing up the Houses of Parliament while King James was inside. The plot didn't work and the British have been celebrating the fact ever since. Each November kids all over the British Isles and former British colonies build huge bonfires and let off fireworks to celebrate the foiling of the Gunpowder Plot. "Remember, remember, the fifth of November" is a cry that's heard all over, starting somewhere in October.

This November my school friends and I had plans to attend Robert Oakes's bonfire, just down the street from the house I was staying in for the weekend, so it was very handy. I hurriedly ate supper, said goodbye to Maud Hall, the lady I was staying with, and went off to join my friends, sparklers in hand. All the big fireworks would be handled by the adults, but we kids were allowed to bring sparklers.

We were having a lot of fun watching the fireworks and dancing around the bonfire, but as often happens when kids are left to their own devices, things got out of hand. The adults had gone inside to cool off and have a beer, leaving us kids outside to watch the dying bonfire.

There's one in every crowd. Some kid who wants to be daring and show off to his pals. Dudley Asquith was ours. He had taken an old bicycle tyre and cut it, so that it was this long, curved piece of rubber, and he had laid one end of it in the dying bonfire, where it had, of course, caught fire.

Dudley dared us all to play jump-the-burning-tyre, and started swinging the tyre slowly in a circle. Most of the kids were too smart to fall for his dare, but one of the boys gave it a try and jumped over the flaming tyre as it swung slowly in a circle. Since he came out of it okay, I decided to try it, too. I didn't take into account the fact that this boy was older and taller than I was.

Dudley swung the tyre again and I jumped over it, feeling elated because I made it safely. But for our next turns, Dudley decided to do some fancy swinging and made the burning tyre go up and down, like a snake, as well as going around. I misjudged the distance and as I jumped, the burning end of the tyre hit me smack on my bare legs.

My screams brought all the adults running.

The Fire Department was called and I was rushed to the Fire Station where they could treat my burns. Before they could do that they had to get all the melted black rubber off. I'll never forget the way they methodically scraped that stuff from my legs, as I screamed like a banshee.

They must have done a terrific job of getting most of the rubber off, because all I have to show for the experience is a small scar on the inside of my right leg, just below the knee.

I wonder if that's the reason I am so anti-practical jokes and stupidly dangerous stunts as an adult? Could be.

Anyway, Mum's job didn't work out as she'd hoped, so she moved back to Sydney for a while, to review her options. I was sent back to Sydney in the train, Pat moved back home and Dad, Mum, Pat, and I stayed in our nice cozy house for quite some time after that.

Until our next adventure.

MISSED MOMENTS

by Linda Noble

As I was watching the game show, *Wheel of Fortune*, which was being broadcast from Disneyland last night, they showed a shot of the Electrical Parade, marching down Main Street - and it took me back 30 years.

We were there, tired after traipsing around Disneyland all day, weary with the children being so young and energetic, utterly worn out from taking turns carrying the children on our shoulders. I looked around at the people without children hanging on their arms. They seemed to be having so much fun. They laughed, talked, and pointed expectantly, as the distant parade came slowly closer in the soft, California night.

John and Jane felt the excitement of the crowd and began to get agitated again. Even their big brother, Rick, who was 14 at the time, couldn't quiet them down. Besides, he was almost as tired as we were. "I can't see!" "Lift me up!" the younger ones demanded. When we lifted them onto our aching shoulders again, it was "I wanna go to the bathroom!" from John, 4, and "Mommy, I firsty!" from Jane, 1-1/2 years old.

Those childless people were still there, glancing at us with that half-compassionate look that says, "I feel sorry for you, but I'm glad I'm not you." They looked sophisticated, suave, cosmopolitan, cool, and fresh. All the things I wanted to be, but couldn't. Not with chocolate from Jane's ice cream cone dripping down her chin into my hair. Not with John throwing himself from side to side on his father's shoulders, making me dizzy just watching him. I sighed a deep sigh as the parade moved right in front of us and the kids stared in awe, quiet for a moment at last. Soon, I said to myself. Soon they'll be older.

How right I was. So soon it made my head spin. Looking back over the years that have sped by, the dismal thought occurs to me that I missed much of my children's childhood. Not physically, but mentally. Oh, I was there all right, begrudging many moments like the one at Disneyland, wishing they were old enough to take care of themselves, so I could have some fun.

Well. They're old enough now. Unfortunately, I realized too late that the fun was there all the time.

Now, when I see little kids, their eyes full of curiosity, their faces full of wonder and chocolate – still chocolate – I think of all the funny expressions I'll never see on my children's faces. All the moments of dawning as they look at something completely new to them. The open-mouthed drooly stares as they see something they've never seen before.

I should have looked more closely, while I could.

BANGKOK, THAILAND

by Linda Noble

The first sight of Bangkok is silver and green
rice paddies and rivers, looking serene.
Long threads of water; like worms after rain.
glisten in the sunshine from high in the plane.

The old airport building is filled with sound:
incomprehensible announcements resound;
The bells, and the bangs and the clatter of bags
There's people in suits and there's people in rags.

The strong smell of flowers and luggage and sweat
make a unique aroma I'll never forget.

Little brown faces, slashed with big grins
offer leis and their sales pitches add to the din..
These children are ten, or eleven, or twelve
but they look so much older - like little old elves.

The leis can be had for a price that's agreed
and the money they get, the kids pocket with speed.

While children are wheedling and selling their wares,
the old battered taxis are waiting for fares.
For the most part they're broken-down, rusty old
   crates -
they look like they couldn't hold very much weight.

But somehow they make it, God only knows how,
while the white-knuckled tourists, with sweat on
   their brow
look decidedly ashen, as the cabs shake and rock,
Sawaddi, kha, Foreigner - Welcome to Bangkok!

LUCILLE DOESN'T LIVE HERE ANYMORE

by Linda Noble

The nurse's starched uniform rustled as she hurried by. She stopped at the door of 304 to look in on her favorite patient, only to find that Lucille's daughter, Mrs. Miller, was sitting beside Lucille's bed pouring out her troubles again. The nurse shook her head and continued on to the nurses' station.

"What's the matter, Grady? Is it the battleaxe again?" Jill Grady's friend, the charge nurse said softly.

"I don't know why that woman bothers me so much, Liz. I guess having your family come to see you is better than being neglected."

"In this case, I'm not so sure," Liz responded. "All she ever seems to do is complain and tell her mother all of *her* problems - as if she doesn't have enough of her own to worry about."

Jill gazed out the window at the snow eddying about. "I'm not so sure she worries at all, to tell you the truth," she said. "I watch her face when I'm taking vitals and bathing her. Her face is SO calm and peaceful. I often wonder where her mind is."

*   *   *   *

The sun is shining so beautifully. It feels warm on my hand. I can see thousands of dust motes dancing in that sunbeam streaming through the window pane. Mama would be mortified if she thought there was any dust in our house, but I love it! I can hear the old grandfather clock, ticking *away, and, if I tilt my head - just so - I can see myself in the mirror above the hearth. Mama says I shouldn't be vain, but my new dress is **so** pretty and the ribbon in my hair looks **just right** today. The curls fall right from the top of my head alllll the way down my back.*

*   *   *   *

"Michael and I are entitled to a life for ourselves, you know. MoTHER! You do understand don't you? I wish you'd at least answer me sometimes. I take time out of my week to come and sit here talking to you, the least you could do is respond. Well, hopefully the people at the nursing home will bring you out of this...this...whatever it is. As I was telling you in the car just before the accident, I've heard that nursing home is very nice. People usually have to go on a waiting list to get in, but of course, since I'm the president of...."

*   *   *   *

Mmmmm. Warm sunshine. I almost went to sleep a minute ago, but then I caught Daddy's eye - and he winked at me! Soon that lady will finish talking and leave - then Daddy and I can play hide-and-go-seek. There's so many wonderful places to hide in our house. Daddy even showed me a secret passage! Now I can fool everybody when it's my turn to hide - everybody but Daddy, that is!

*   *   *   *

"...so now that Cassie's out of college and moving to New York, Michael and I thought we'd get a smaller place. We don't need four bedrooms anymore. And of course, once we get you out of this hospital and into 'Golden Hills' we'll only need a little one-bedroom apartment. I think that ridiculous affair of Michael's is finally over - thank the Lord! With the children gone and time to spend with each other, we'll be fine! Why, just the other day..."

Jill Grady stood outside Lucille's room for a moment, listening to Mrs. Miller go on and on. She remembered the night they had brought Lucille in. Her face had been haggard with pain, and she was crying. Not just tears running down her face, but heart wrenching sobs that racked her frail body. Jill was a hardened nurse; she'd just about seen it all, but something about Lucille tore at her heart and she had to concentrate hard not to cry herself.

Lucille was the victim of a car accident. Her daughter had been driving and had escaped unharmed. Jennifer Miller had lost control of her car while talking on her cell phone and, sliding around on the icy road, had crashed into a telephone pole, pinning Lucille into the front passenger seat, crushing her legs.

After the first surgery, when they realized how badly damaged Lucille's legs were, the doctors had waited for her to come out of recovery so they could talk to her about the possibility of a prosthesis for her right leg, which was twisted beyond repair. But they were never able to discuss it with their patient. Lucille had awakened from her drug-induced sleep all right, but had not uttered a word, then, or since.

Instead of the distraught woman who had been admitted that first night, there had been only calmness and quiet; no response to questions, no crying, no accelerated heartbeat--nothing. Although Lucille was not technically in a coma, she was just as unreachable. She would sit, propped up on pillows, with her eyes open, seemingly awake. Sometimes, she would even look directly at whomever was with her, but if one looked closely it was obvious that Lucille wasn't present, mentally.

The doctors had patched up her physical injuries as well as they could, but did not seem able to penetrate her mind at all. Even though Lucille would probably never walk again, her general health was good; so there seemed to be no medical reason why she would not come back to the land of the living.

The hospital staff was understandably concerned about Lucille-- particularly Jill, who spent a lot of time with her. When she had heard of Lucille's plight, Jill's 9-year old daughter, Mandy, had insisted on sending one of her favorite stuffed toys to Lucille, saying that *nobody* could ignore Toto, her ragged little terrier with the infectious, though fixed, grin. Unfortunately, Toto had failed to work his magic this time and he still lay on Lucille's bed, untouched.

*   *   *   *

"Thank you, Mommy! Oh, it's so beautiful!" I have the BEST Mommy in the world! Wait until I see Susan Farnham tomorrow - she's going to be so envious! A real, live puppy for my birthday! Oh, he's SO adorable!

*   *   *   *

"...Of course we're going to have to put Rusty to sleep. It's hard enough to find a decent apartment these days - let alone one that will take animals! Now, Mother, don't look at me like that. It's not as if he's in very good health - is it? He's old and he can hardly walk anymore... Are you listening to me, Mother?"

Jill listened with one ear as Mrs. Miller droned on. She was sitting at the nurse's station filling in her daily report, and even at this distance the woman's voice could be heard clearly. Jill propped her head on her hands, elbows resting on the desk. She felt more depressed than usual today. She rubbed her eyes, thinking about the end of her shift when she could go home. She was exhausted after working double shifts all week, and was looking forward to being able to drop into bed. She felt as though she could sleep for a week.

As Jill opened her eyes and looked up she was suddenly shocked out of her lethargy. She saw Lucille standing right in front of her! Jill's head snapped back and her eyes widened as she stared at Lucille who was smiling at her, and she had Toto in her hand. Slowly, Lucille raised the hand holding the toy, extending it toward Jill. Although no words came out, Lucille's mouth formed the words, "Thank you," and she smiled again. Jill shook her head to clear it, thinking she must be dreaming. When she opened her eyes again, Lucille was not there.

An alarmed voice rang out, coming from Lucille's room.

"Nurse! NURSE! Where is that *damned* nurse when you need her? There's something wrong with my mother! With what we're paying in this place, you'd think there'd be a nurse around when you need one!" Mrs. Miller appeared at the nurses' station, looking flustered.

"There you are!"

Jill ran into the room, and her heart skipped a beat as she saw Lucille slumped down in the bed, eyes closed, looking very pale. Mrs. Miller was talking nervously.

"It was the strangest thing. I was talking to her and suddenly she just looked at me, no words or anything, then she just turned her face away from me and I saw her body relax, as though she was asleep. I kept calling her, and finally..." Jill was only half listening to Mrs. Miller as she searched for a pulse. No pulse. No evidence of breathing.

Ignoring Mrs. Miller's whining voice, Jill ran to the nurse's station to use the PA and get a doctor there, STAT. Her hand shook as she held the microphone. After making the announcement Jill turned to run back to Lucille's room when her foot brushed against something in the corridor. She looked down and froze. The little toy dog that had been sitting on Lucille's bed all these weeks was lying on the floor in front of the nurse's station - right where Lucille had left it.

JAKARTA

by Linda Noble

The busy Jakarta airport was left behind as our car pulled away with a squeal of tires. The driver kept looking back at us, smiling at everyone, nodding his head, and giving a little giggle every time one of us returned his smile. I was wishing he would pay as much attention to the terrifying traffic that surrounded us as he was to being charming.

Cars, buses, strange looking three-wheeled vehicles, motor cycles, hand-pulled rickshaws (which I later learned were called betjaks) were everywhere, most of them spitting out black, noxious smoke and loud screeching blasts of horns, in equal amounts. We finally figured out that if we looked away from the driver, he stopped nodding and smiling at us. He obviously felt obliged to keep up his end of things, as the sole member of our welcoming committee.

Our first impression of Jakarta was remarkable. There seemed to be constant chaotic movement. Dodging in and out among all the fast-moving vehicles were scores of people of all ages. From old men to children, they had one thing in common - they were agile; they had to be to dodge *that* traffic.

Old men, each carrying a long, bamboo stick on his shoulders, with a basket on each end, shuffled along the streets. The men had an unusual gait - keeping their shoulders quite still, yet moving their lower bodies very quickly. While their legs pumped away, their upper bodies hardly moved at all, allowing whatever was in the baskets to remain in them.

Some of the men had bare chests, some wore old, open-necked shirts, and some wore the more traditional sarongs. Almost all of the tukangs (vendors) wore little black hats with a tassel bobbing from the crown, sort of like a squashed fez. Each had different goods for sale - from statues of elephants to wayang goleks, which are tall, elaborately-dressed puppets with brightly-colored faces.

The skin on the men's faces was dark and leathery, lined through many years of squinting in the sun. They all had huge smiles showing stained teeth - and gaps where teeth used to be. Many of them had skinny cigarettes dangling from their lower lips, defying gravity, as the men hurried along.

The women stayed on the perimeter of the major roads, sitting at makeshift stalls on crumbling sidewalks, selling dozens of food items. Many were selling sateh, the Indonesian version of shish kabob (but made from goat meat, which smelled absolutely wonderful!) There were also sticky-looking, thick drinks in small glasses, which we later found to be very tasty iced coffee.

Again, their manner of dress varied from Western clothes to batik sarongs. With their sarong-type long skirts, most of the women wore tops made of brightly-colored lace, with long sleeves and a collar. The colors were different, but the style always seemed to be the same.

For the most part, the women wore their hair up, fastened back from their faces with decorative combs. They seemed to be constantly chewing and, when I smiled at one of them and she smiled back, I noticed with dismay that her teeth were red! It turns out that betel nuts were the culprit. Many Indonesians chew them as we would chew gum. After years of doing this, nothing would get that red stain off their teeth. It looked ghoulish, to say the least.

Children swarmed everywhere. They were all wiry, dark-skinned little urchins with ready smiles and wisdom in their eyes beyond their years. They were selling things, too. Each had arms full of beautiful, strongly-scented, flower leis for sale. The boys were the more adventurous, ducking in and out of the traffic, grinning impishly when brakes were applied hurriedly and horns sounded. Then they would shinny up a lamp post to scout out their next customers.

The girls ran with the boys, but seemed more reserved. As we stopped for a red light, several of them surrounded the car, holding up their leis, grinning, and holding up five fingers. The driver turned and asked in his broken English, if we wanted some leis. When we said yes, he rolled down the window of the car and the blast of hot air made us really appreciate the car's air conditioning.

As well as letting in the hot air, the sounds from outside were suddenly much louder; there were shouts, horns blaring, tires screeching and what sounded like about 50 radios – all blaring out music. Unfortunately, they were not all tuned to the same station, which made for an unbelievable racket.

Even so, I looked around with pleasure and anticipation at this exciting place that was to be our home for the next three years.

A DELLMAN RIDE TO THE MARKET

by Linda Noble
from Jane's perspective

When we lived in Indonesia we would often ride to the marketplace in town. Sometimes we would take the car and driver, sometimes a betjak (a vehicle that looks like a large bicycle with a huge seat on the front where the passengers would sit). But our favorite way to go was by Dellman - a horse and carriage, but the carriage faces backwards, so you were looking at where you'd been instead of where you were going.

My family was in Bogor, Indonesia, with my dad, who was a chemical engineer with a tire company. We had a lot of fun there, because there was so much to do. We could go the guesthouse to swim, eat, and play games with our friends, or we could take trips up to the mountains, or climb trees, or go to the market place.

Our maid, Hayati, would come along to do any bargaining for us, because although John and I, and just about all the expatriate kids, spoke Indonesian, it wasn't good enough for detailed conversations.

Shopping was different over there. They *expected* everyone to bargain for whatever they bought. The vendors would start at a really high price, and we would start at a really low price, and we'd usually end up at a price somewhere in the middle. Our older brother, Rick, was the best at it in our family, but he had longer school hours than John and me, so we often went along with Hayati instead.

Dellman rides are wonderful! We'd sit up high on the wooden seats, where we had a good view of everything and everyone. The horses would just plod along and the rhythm of their hoofs made a cool sound on the asphalt streets.

Hayati would bargain with the driver to take us into town and there we'd be, in our own little private carriage looking at all the sights. First we'd drive down *Jalan Gunung Gede* (Big Mountain Street) where there were huge old trees, their branches spreading over the road, making it like a green archway over the street. Most of the people on the streets knew us, and waved to us as we rode by.

We'd drive past Hayati's *campung* (village) where her whole family lived. She would sometimes take us home with her and we'd go through dozens of narrow, winding streets till we got to her house. Even though we knew which one it was, Hayati would point it out excitedly each time we came close. She didn't speak much English, but we spoke enough Indonesian to get by, so we understood each other perfectly.

We'd pass the Bata Shoe Store where Mom would take us all to get new shoes, and the little grocery store where we bought tea and sugar and flour and things. Next door to Bata was a little restaurant owned by a friend of my parents, and whenever we'd go in there, he'd make us eat frogs' legs cooked in garlic that were delicious. Actually, it tasted pretty much like chicken; the legs were just smaller.

You always knew when you were getting close to the market. There were hundreds of people moving around all the stalls and it had its own special smell - something like all kinds of vegetables together, mixed with spices, and meat, overlaid with the heavy smell of animal droppings. Yum.

When Hayati paid the Dellman driver, we'd start at one side of the market and slowly work our way - winding back and forth - to the other end. There was music playing through loud speakers all the time. The one I remember the most was The Carpenters singing their big hit, "*Sing.*" The Carpenters were very popular in Indonesia.

We never bought very much; just looked at everything – all the clothes and the animals, and food for sale. Sometimes Hayati would buy us one of the little toys we saw.

Not being used to seeing blonde hair, we would get stopped dozens of times by people wanting to touch our hair. We got used to it.

When we were done walking around the market place, we'd go back to the street and find another Dellman and ride home again to see Mom and play in our garden.

My brothers and I had lots of fun in Indonesia.

LEAPIN LIZARDS!

by Linda Noble

Jane's scream wasn't exactly blood-curdling, but enough to make us all pay attention. There she stood, by the door, eyes tightly shut, arms held stiffly at her sides, looking terrified. Jane was fond of histrionics, so we didn't usually react too violently to her screams. This time, though, she had a decent reason. There was a pale green, almost see-through lizard running down her dress! When it reached the hem of her dress it made a tremendous jump - for something only three inches long - to the ground, and scurried off under the bed. We were all stunned, but Haman, the houseboy, who was helping us move into the guesthouse, just laughed.

"Oh, Little Missy," he said to Jane, "Don't you worry 'bout that little thing. He won' hurt you."

"I hope somebody told *him* that!" she answered, her voice shaking.

Haman laughed again. "They called chin-chuks. Eats all the bugs and spiders. We never have spiders here at Guesthouse - not for very long anyway!"

Here we were, in Indonesia, a long way from home, and practically the first creature we meet is a horrible-looking lizard! My husband's company forgot to tell us we'd be expected to cohabit with reptiles when they transferred him to Bogor.

Our headquarters were in Akron, Ohio, but since the company's Indonesian plant needed a new chief chemist, and my husband had the experience they needed, he was it. It looked as though life in Bogor, Indonesia, was going to be *quite* a bit different from life in Akron.

"Are there...many of those, er..." I began.

"Chin-chuks, Madame," he laughed again. Indonesians certainly are a happy race of people - always laughing.

"You know how many fishes in the sea?" he asked me with a big grin.

"Well, that's how many chin-chuks we got," his grin widened, "in the Guesthouse!" he finished, grinning widely, obviously enjoying himself.

"COOL!" said John, who is three years older than Jane. "Can we keep 'em?"

"Tell you what, Young Tuan, you can keep as many as you can catch!" This time Haman's laughter boomed out.

As we set our bags down on the bedroom floor, we all looked around warily. Sure enough, there on the bedroom wall, high up, was a chin-chuk. He was about five feet away from a mosquito. Quick as a flash, the lizard made his move. He covered the five feet in no time flat, flicked out his tongue, scooped up the mosquito, and darted back to who-knows-where!

"It looks as though they're under the board that runs around the ceiling," my husband remarked, craning his neck to try to see under the board.

"Tuan (the Indonesian version of Mister), they EVERYWHERE!" Haman replied, laughing again.

"Well, hon., it looks like we'll have to learn to live with them," my husband said cheerfully.

Jane and I both gave him an 'easy-for-you-to-say' look. Still, it wasn't as though we could do anything about it. It seemed the lizards were there to stay, and so were we - for three years, anyway.

* * * *

Actually, lizards notwithstanding, Indonesia turned out to be a pretty good place to live. Rick was 14, John, 12, and Jane 9, so they all had different outside interests. Much to their disappointment, they still had to go to school! I think they'd had visions dancing in their heads of skipping school - just because the nearest English-speaking school was 60 Kms (almost 40 miles) away. But a company driver took all the expatriate children back and forth to Jakarta to school. By the time they got back in the afternoon, they couldn't wait to change clothes and go do something that was fun.

One of Rick's favorite pastimes was climbing the papaya trees in our back yard. The trunks were very tall and skinny, and for the most part, bare. The branches didn't appear until the very top of the tree - then they grew directly out of the top, complete with large leaves and heavy, delicious fruits that were yellow on the outside and a delicate pink inside.

"O.K., Haman. Give me another chance. I'm *sure* I can beat you this time!" Rick yelled, still out of breath from the last effort.

"You want me to let you win?" Haman asked jokingly.

"NO! You won't need to, anyway - I'm getting faster all the time."

It was true. After two years, 16-year old Rick had become very agile, but he had yet to beat Haman who, although he was much older than Rick - Haman was an 'old' man of 30 - had been climbing these trees all of his life.

I watched as the race started over again, surprised that all the bark hadn't been worn off the trees long ago. It had taken Rick ages to adopt the method of the native tree climbers - with a foot on either side of the tree, knees bent, bare feet gripping the tree's sides, and holding onto the trunk with both hands, so that when they moved, they were literally running up the trunk of the tree, holding on with hands and feet.

While Rick was busy climbing, John was discovering how much he loved horses. He was lucky enough to have a friend who lived a few houses away with a yard big enough to keep horses. John and Andre would change their clothes the minute they got home from school and go riding until dark. Or sometimes there would be a baseball game in the nearby park, with a group of expatriate children and a growing group of laughing native children who picked up the game very quickly considering they had never seen a real baseball game.

Jane would rather shop than just about anything! She and I would often go into town in a dellman (horse and carriage) and wander around the market place where there were interesting sights and sounds - and smells. Everything from live animals to clothes and jewelry were available in the maze of passageways that made up the local market.

For about the first year, Jane had been afraid of the hordes of chin-chuks that invaded everyone's houses. Haman had been right - they *were* everywhere. They would lie in wait above the doorways, then would let go their little suction-cupped feet and drop onto whoever happened to be walking through. I swear they made a game of it. Probably handed out blue ribbons to the one who dive bombed the most humans! Strangely enough though, we got so used to them we hardly noticed anymore.

After the first year, Jane had learned to tolerate them, although I think the main reason was that she was so thankful because they kept the enormous insect population down. As time went on, she could even walk through a doorway and simply brush the little creatures off her shoulder, and they would scurry away and run back up the wall, to jump on the next unsuspecting victim.

Whether taking a dellman to the crowded, colorful market, or traveling up to the nearby mountains to sample some local Javanese taste treats, living in Indonesia was quite an experience. Time passed much too quickly. Almost before we knew it, our 3-year assignment was up, the Indonesian plant was operating well under the management of the local people my husband had trained, and it was time to go back home.

As it got closer to the time to return to the States, I realized that I was going to miss this place where my children had grown so tall and where we'd all learned so much. A country of lush, tropical scenery, daily cooling rain showers, and spicy, delicious foods.

But most of all, we'd miss the smiling faces of the friendly Indonesian people who helped make our transition from 'green' foreigners to residents, so pleasant. We had learned some of the language, some of the customs, and a lot of the folklore, and in the process had made some friends.

Just before we left Bogor, we were showing the family of my husband's replacement around the guesthouse. They were all wide-eyed, as we had been. Suddenly, there was a screech from their 11-year old daughter, Sarah, as a chin-chuk landed, splat, on her head. Sarah looked scared out of her wits, but I knew we'd made it as honorary natives when Jane said: "Oh, don't worry about them. They're just chin-chuks - they won't hurt you," and she winked at Haman and laughed.

SPICY SOUP!

by Linda Noble

When Charlie MacDonald said he was working late Margie knew it meant he would be with his girlfriend. Margie had seen her once, and was amazed and ashamed that she was not much older than their own daughters. For years it had been tacitly understood that he would not flaunt his affairs and she would ignore them. This latest one though, was different. She called him every night, right at dinner time, in the presence of her daughters.

Margie tried to maintain the illusion that she and Charlie had a good marriage, but the girls knew better. All the years they'd been growing up they'd been subjected to their father's constant humiliation of their mother. It was always, "Margie, don't you have another outfit to wear? That one is hideous!" or "As usual, this soup is too bland - have you ever heard of spices, Margie?" or "For heavens sake, fix your hair!"

Just last night, on one of the few days this week Charlie had been home for dinner, Margie detected a 'look' that passed between the girls as Charlie got up from the table to answer the phone. Margie had felt a hot flush spread from her neck over her whole face. A few minutes later it had been "...out for a while...emergency at the office..." from Charlie.

And now, here she was again, sitting at the dinner table alone. The girls were spending the night with Rachel Evans, a friend from their high school days. Charlie was on the phone, talking softly, intimately. Faintly, she could hear the theme music for *Night Court* from the TV the girls had left on. She didn't bother to turn the set off, she just sat silently, not eating, staring out of the window at the sunset.

Charlie finally rejoined her at the table, and picked up his soup spoon. As he took his first sip, he looked up in surprise.

"Well, Margie, you finally made the soup spicy enough! It's about time."

She watched him eat, her eyes following the spoon from the bowl to Charlie's mouth. She cleared the soup bowls and brought in the main course. They ate in silence.

Charlie picked up his newspaper and settled in the big armchair to read, while Margie did the dishes and cleaned up the kitchen. At nine o'clock Charlie yawned and went upstairs to the bedroom. Margie stayed in front of the TV with a strong bourbon by her side, watching the antics of Ms. Murphy Brown, whom she admired very much.

She heard Charlie moving around, getting ready for bed, and finally the bed creaked as he lay down. Margie looked toward the ceiling with a little smile on her face and said, in a matter of fact voice: "I'm glad you liked the soup, dear, but I'm afraid I'm going to have to renew my valium prescription tomorrow. You see, I used the last of it today."

Margie picked up her drink, silently toasted her husband of 25 years, and went back to watching the show.

METAMORPHOSIS

by Linda Noble

How is it that people change so drastically when the parent/child roles are finally reversed? We start out doing as Mom or Dad says because they're our authority figures. There are many years where we wouldn't dream of disobeying them. Then come the "Wonder Years" - it's a wonder we survive them! We know everything, our parents know nothing. It's a 'wonder' they've made it this long without our enlightened view of things.

Gradually though, we realize that our parents did things, said things, were the way they were because of a set of circumstances, events, and experiences called life. And suddenly, there we are, smack in the middle of life ourselves.

Somewhere in middle age, by the time we've suffered a little, been humiliated enough, and are disillusioned with our earlier ideas of utopia, we come to the sad realization that we *are* our parents. We're not only all-grown-up, but we have kids old enough to drive! We realize our parents worried about the very same things we do: health, finances, kid trouble, world peace, and more.

When we were kids, we pestered and whined and yelled about the center of our universe – us. Mom and Dad always said, "Wait till you have kids of your own! Then you'll know how it feels!" At the time it sounded like a threat. And guess what? It was, because - as the popular expression goes - what goes around, comes around.

We seem to go from changing diapers to changing plans, overnight ("Mom, can my new friends stay for dinner?" "Dad, can we borrow your car? I promise we won't smash it like last time!" "Mom, we won't be there for dinner after all - I forgot we were gonna go somewhere!")

And of course kids think we're made of money. They have no idea how finances work - that you have to save some money out of every paycheck to allow for a rainy day (like paying for the damages when one of your teenagers wrecks the car!) You're so busy being thankful they're okay that you hardly even notice it cleaned out your tiny balance.

Your bills have mounted up to the point that even with both of you working it's tough to make ends meet. Your younger teenager (the one who *hasn't* wrecked the car yet) turns to you one day and says, "Why can't I have a new prom dress! Everyone else is buying a new one and you want me to go to *Goodwill* for a second-hand one?! You don't care about me at all!" and she runs off in tears. Sigh. You're torn between smacking her one and putting your arms around her and crying with her.

But these things, too, come to pass and before you know it, your kids are all grown up, out of the house, and it's just you, your spouse and the dog. You're congratulating yourselves on having raised your brood; they've worked out their earlier problems in the process of getting older themselves. You finally have a little money to spend on yourselves and you're enjoying being grandparents - parenthood without all the problems. Then bang! It's time for the next major change of your life.

One of your parents has died and the other is not able to take care of him or herself. Where does the parent go? Why, he/she moves in with you two and the dog, of course.

This is when things get hairy again. At some point we begin treating them like children: "Mother, did you change your underwear today?" Or we snap at them for minor infractions such as asking you to repeat something they may not have understood, or even something as minor as meandering down memory lane. "Oh, Gram, that's not the way it was at all. You *always* say that!"

Soon we start to resent the fact that our parents are tying us down. We can't go somewhere because Grandma or Grandpa (most often, they're relegated to these titles now) can't be left alone. This frustration displays itself by us snapping at the offending party. It's not really that we're mad at them. Often it's a way of dealing with the futility we feel because our parents are getting older and more infirm, and there's not a thing we can do about it.

Perhaps the responsibility of the situation scares us, the way it did when our children were little and they depended on us for everything. Or perhaps, subconsciously, it's the realization that we will be in the same position ourselves one of these days.

So we snap, and we pick, and we condescend. But these people who have endured the indignities of life just the same as we have, only longer, deserve better than that. They probably don't want much more than simple respect, and *some* control over their own lives; even if it's only the luxury of being allowed to stay home alone once in a while, so they don't always feel like a ball and chain around your neck.

Something as simple as passing on tips on how to do this or that better/easier/faster makes them feel useful. Having their grandchildren actually listen when they're telling about some long-past event - even if they've heard it before - makes them feel wanted; part of the family. When they state their opinion on something they want people to listen, not pooh-pooh their ideas because they "don't understand." They have a wealth of experience and understanding to share. The problem is finding someone who's willing to let them share.

I'm as guilty as the next person. My mother, bless her heart, lives in Australia - and that's a long way away from Akron, Ohio. Mom has always been an independent cuss; refusing to retire until she was forced to, at the age of 70, by constant lower back pain. Even so, we asked Mom if she'd like to come to the States and live with us.

In her heyday, Mom was an energetic, take-charge person. She was always ready with an opinion whether it was asked for or not. Unfortunately, her daughter is just like her - and back then I still thought I knew everything.

We had tried living in the same house several times and it had never worked before. This last time, 15 years ago, was no exception. Mom was 72. My kids were still young and although I made sure they weren't disrespectful, they never sat down and actually talked with my mother. They don't know her at all. They were too busy with sports, school, dances, and friends, to spend time with Nana.

I was no better. It seemed that every time she wanted to talk was the 'wrong' time for me. I was busy - on my way to work, home from work, fixing dinner, heading for a meeting/rehearsal/errand - you name it, there was always an excuse.

When she did get a chance to talk, and because Mom felt the need to still be thought of as sharp, she would replay the scenes of triumph from the days when she was working and leading a 'useful' life.

Or she might criticize the way I was doing some household task saying "Why don't you try it this way?" Sometimes she would emphatically insist that this was so, or that was so, even when talking about things she had no experience with. That can be very annoying, certainly, but I didn't have to shoot everything she said down in flames. I could at least have tried to take what she was saying under consideration.

So she didn't know about the subject but had an opinion anyway. Was that a crime? And who knows? Maybe I *would* find her way of doing something easier/faster/better. And even if Mom was wrong, did I have to let her know about it every time? Apparently so. Sad, isn't it.

So Mom went back to Australia because she was having medical problems and wanted her own doctor. She missed the country where she had spent most of her life, and we certainly hadn't gone out of our way to make her feel an integral part of our lives.

Now she's too old to travel and I only see her once in a blue moon when my husband and I manage to save up the roundtrip fare to Australia (once in the last 15 years). She's always happy to see me and I'm always happy to see her. But the tears come readily to my eyes when I see her these days. She looks so old and frail.

Would it have hurt me to let her ramble on instead of cutting her short? Would it have killed me to tell her that some method she had tried to push on me worked better than my method?

Neglect and failure to listen are not the only sins we wreak on the elderly. When I see people talk to their parents as though they were children I cringe. "Sit *down*, mother! You know you can't do that anymore!" "Dad, when will you learn to flush the toilet after yourself?" "We can't come because Grandpa can't be left alone," and on, and on...

I hope my children treat me better than that when my time comes.

A LESSON LEARNED?

by Linda Noble

I wasn't the only one who was appalled at the way Karen Berger treated her servants. We all were. We often said to each other things like, "How would you feel if you were searched every night before you left your job," or "Imagine being yelled at and made to feel a fool in front of your co-workers!" or "Can you believe she takes money from their salaries for a missing spoonful of coffee?"

There were about ten American families living in a little town on the Indonesian island of Java - "all in the same boat," people were fond of saying. I wouldn't say quite the *same* boat. The only similarity was that all of our husbands worked for the same company. Karen and Klaus's 'boat' was decidedly larger, fancier, and definitely more expensive than any of ours.

The Bergers had beautiful, thick carpeting all the way through their fifteen-room home – even in the bathrooms! Their living room was huge. It had an aquarium that ran the length of one wall, with beautiful tropical fish, greenery, rocks and special lighting. The leather-and-teak bar at one end of the room seated ten people comfortably, and occasional tables with glass tops as well as soft, comfy sofas blended beautifully with the objets d'art to make one of the most fabulous rooms I've ever seen. And that was just one room.

With a house that size, there naturally had to be plenty of servants. After all, how would it look if the underlings had as many servants as the Director of Sales? So the Bergers had no less than 10 servants: a cook; two baby babus (one to take care of each of their two children);

two cleaning babus; a houseboy; a laundry babu; a gardener; a driver; and a guard. And we all felt she treated them abominably.

I was in trouble right off the bat. When everyone told me I had to have a bunch of servants I asked how much I needed to pay them, but nobody would give me an actual figure. They'd say things like, "Weeeellll, it depends," or "Different people pay different salaries." So I went straight to the source.

Servants would come to my door looking for work – they all knew there were new *bule bule* (whiteys) in town – and I asked them how much they wanted. When they told me they were looking for a salary equivalent to about ten American dollars a month I about flipped. How could anyone live on $10 a month? I soon found out that not only did they live on it, but they were keeping the rest of their families on it, too.

When the other expatriates' servants started complaining about how they needed more money I got my second big shock. The other expats were paying them even less than that! So the wives chivvied me about overpaying. Too bad, I said. You wouldn't tell me how much to pay them, so I asked the servants what they wanted, and it seemed so little I didn't even hesitate before hiring them.

Karen complained the loudest, of course, even though her servants never uttered a peep about wanting a raise. But in spite of all the brouhaha about the new, crazy *bule* madame - me - Karen was still the biggest topic of conversation.

Karen was a real Tartar - everyone said so. She had a loud and raucous voice that made strong men quake. She was German and although she spoke English fluently, it was heavily accented - and nasal. Still, to her credit, she was a very good mimic and picked up the Indonesian language in no time. Somehow it seemed even worse when she would haul one of her servants over the coals in their own language. Her most constant gripe was that our servants stole from us.

Certainly, stealing is no minor offense, but the rest of us figured that these people were so much poorer than us, that we turned a blind eye to the daily pilfering of food. Not Karen. She had long ago measured exactly how many tablespoons of coffee and sugar went into a pound and how many cups there were in a five-pound bag of flour. Since the female servants wore sarongs, which were bunched around the waistline, and which Karen thought was a perfect hiding place, they were forced to take off their sarongs to prove they were not hiding anything of Karen's, before they left her house every night.

How humiliating, we all said; how dreadful! If one towel went missing and she questioned and searched the staff and couldn't find it, she would dock everyone's pay for the full cost of the towel. The stray towel, or any other household item, turned up "pretty damned quick" as she delighted in telling anyone who'd listen.

The rest of us tended to treat our servants with respect and trust. I, particularly, being young and trusting and completely inexperienced in dealing with servants, began to feel as though my staff were almost part of the family. I became friendly with them, asking about their homes and children, giving them everything my children grew out of, buying them new clothes or shoes when I saw that what they were wearing was old. All seven of my staff had enormous loans from me, and at Ramadan time, their biggest holiday of the year when employers gave gifts to their people, I wiped out their loans as well as giving them money and buying them clothes for their 3-day festival.

Not Karen. If her servants ever dared try to talk to her about something personal - a problem, sick child, etc., she would look them right in the eye and say, "I don't care. Finish your work." She was a hard woman all right.

My servants would tell me what a wonderful Madame I was (not like that horrible Mrs. Berger). Strangers would come to my door asking for employment. They had heard what a "good madame" I was, and begged to be taken onto the payroll. I was definitely in demand as an employer.

Our houseboy's name was Isa (pronounced Eesa) and we all loved him. He was always there when we needed him - changing light bulbs, answering the door and phone, playing with the children, serving meals. And he always had a big smile. I came to trust him so much that I gave him the money to do the daily shopping - more to make him feel important than anything else. For when he showed up at the marketplace with all that money and obviously the trust of the Tuan and Madame, it gave him 'face.' I guess I knew all along that he was getting much better prices than he told me and pocketing the difference; I just didn't want to think about it.

Karen out-and-out told me I was an idiot, soft in the head. I tried to drum some sense of humanity into her by insisting that if you treat people with respect, it will be returned. Karen said, "My servants respect me - look at them!" I did look at them, cowering in the background, smiling ingratiatingly at their Madame, with fear in their eyes. "They don't respect you," I retorted, "They're afraid of you." "Same thing!" she boomed.

I gradually noticed that my servants were taking me for granted, taking more and more days off for all kinds of reasons. At first I was sympathetic, giving them extra food to take to the wake of the loved one who had died (this was the most common excuse). It wasn't until the same maid's grandmother had died twice that I began to complain.

"Oh, but Madame, you so sweet, you best madame in town. You maybe made mistake and think I said grandmother last time, but I said grandfather." Hmmm. These excuses were so frequent that rather than trust my memory, I started writing them down and had it in black and white that this girl's grandmother had died three times and the other staff's ancestors had passed on twice each!

They started getting sloppy. I'd catch them sleeping on the job, laying around talking, with the work not done, whenever I came home unexpectedly. When you have seven servants, you don't expect to have to dust the furniture.

Things began to disappear. "I don't know where it is Madame. Maybe you loaned it to someone?" or "Oh, so sorry the pitcher gone Madame, the dog knocked it off the counter and it broke. We had to throw it out."

At first I believed them, but in the end they weren't even trying to sound sincere. They'd give me some cockamamie excuse and look me right in the eye, as though challenging me to say something about it. Also, they began to have moods. One maid in particular would snap at me if I even looked at her. And more things disappeared.

The final straw was the shoes. I had noticed the soles were coming off the houseboy's tennis shoes, so gave him some money and sent him downtown with our driver to get a new pair. He came back wearing them proudly and handed me the receipt from the Bata store. The amount written on the receipt had been changed in such a clumsy and obvious way that it made me furious. It wasn't even in the same color ink! I asked him what happened. He said the salesman had made a mistake.

By this time, I was fed up with being Mrs. Niceguy. I took Isa and the receipt straight to the car, there and then, and we drove to the Bata shoe store. I showed the salesman the receipt and asked him how much the shoes actually had cost, and of course, Isa had changed it - to the tune of several thousand rupiahs - only a few dollars worth, but suddenly it seemed very important. When we returned home, I fired him. The rest of the servants were speechless.

It didn't end there. I'd had enough. The next time the saucy maid snapped at me, I turned on her and told her if she ever talked to me like that again, she was out on her ear, and that I could get another maid in a twinkling. "Yes, Madame," she said sullenly. I'll show them, I thought. Think I'm stupid, do they? Well, they're in for a surprise. I'm clamping down on all this stealing, sloppy work, and moodiness.

But the problem was, I couldn't maintain that attitude. I had to hand it to Karen - it takes *stamina* to keep up with checking up on seven people every day. And although stealing and lying went against the way I'd been brought up, I just didn't have it in me to keep up a militant facade. After all was said and done, they were *still* damned poor people. I kept thinking what I would do if I had to work for a lousy ten bucks a month! I'd probably steal a few rupiahs too. And how must it look to them for a very healthy looking foreigner - younger than they and twice their size - to need seven people to do everything for her? I think I'd be sullen too.

I went through another metamorphosis then and wanted to get rid of all the servants and do the work myself. I was only 27 years old, and strong as a horse. I almost did it too. However, I found out from my language teacher that the measly sum we were paying our staff kept all of their families, including aunts, uncles and cousins, in relative luxury. He said it would be a very bad thing to let the servants go - so...the status remained more or less 'quo.'

I calmed down after the shoe incident and we all slipped back into our old ways. They took what they wanted, and I let them. I found I really missed Isa's smiling face, but by the time I'd decided to hell with 'losing face' I was going to hire him back anyway, he had been snapped up by another family. So we found another houseboy who wasn't nearly as personable as Isa but who stole just as much, and so, with an unspoken agreement and a wary truce, we finished our 3-year tour of duty.

Funny thing: Karen Berger never lost a thing while she was in Indonesia and she had a wonderful time all the years she and her family lived there. Her servants all went to the airport to see the Bergers off when they finished their assignment - crying real tears and carrying on as though they were losing their best friend. Funny.

THE WEEKEND MARKET

by Linda Noble

For many years, people from all over the world, tourists and residents alike, have thronged to the maze known as the Weekend Market, in Bangkok, Thailand, where you can buy anything from ivory elephants to live insects, ready to eat.

Each tiny, narrow, unbelievably crowded 'street' leads to dozens of other lanes and alleyways. One loses one's direction very quickly, for the Weekend Market is literally the biggest flea market in the world - and probably the only one where you can actually purchase fleas, if you're so inclined!

The constant sound is the first thing you notice: the chittering of monkeys; the rattle of bangles, belt buckles, knives, large tin milk containers; the screech of parrots; the spiels of people selling their wares, each trying to outdo the others in volume and bargains.

The smells add another dimension to this exotic bazaar. The sweet smell of mango and sticky rice, the acrid smell of clove cigarettes. The mouth-watering smell of skewered meat marinated in delicious sauces, cooking on dozens of charcoal grills. The slightly onerous smell of animal droppings, strong perfume, Mekong whiskey, all assail the nostrils.

The array of foodstuffs available is amazing. Over here you'll see a small charcoal stove with a whole squid being turned over and over, browning evenly. Next door will be a wheeled cart made of wood with glass sides, displaying the contents: ducks hanging upside down, featherless but complete with heads; or crispy-looking pig entrails. On another cart there are strange-looking fruits (to those of us brought up on apples and oranges) with unusual smells and flavors.

One fruit, the mangosteen, has a hard purple skin and looks like a petrified mini-eggplant. Once this fruit is cut open you see soft white, clearly-defined sections, almost like grapefruit sections but more definite, and slightly fuzzy, like a peach. The texture is pulpy, slightly chewy, something like a tough marshmallow. Although it is sweet, there is a pervasive sharpness to the fruit, almost like a citrus flavor, but not quite. Full of juice, a mangosteen leaves a deliciously refreshing feeling in your mouth.

Then there's the durian – the emperor of all fruits (according to most Asians, that is). Foreigners have to have very strong stomachs to be able to get it past their noses. Although durian smells like a sewer gone bad, the brave people who have actually eaten this fruit say it's out of this world. Then of course there's the other school of thought that believes it's not far *enough* out of this world.

In spite of its unappetizing traits, Durian is the most expensive fruit in Thailand; it costs ten times what most other fruits cost per kilo. Oval in shape, the skin is covered with big spikes (it looks like a prickly American football). The skin is more like a carapace, and once you get it off, the fruit inside is yellow, not unlike a cantaloupe - in looks, at least. It's a definite delicacy, and as far as this writer is concerned, ranks up there with monkey brains and sheep's eyes in desirability.

The Weekend Market is a unique mix of indoor and outdoor sites. The narrow passages already described are just one part of this huge domain. From within the maze of shops and stalls, a large outside area will suddenly open up, revealing what looks like a sea of enormous beach umbrellas stuck in the ground, creating bits of shade for their owners. After walking through the dim, crowded alleyways, the dazzling sunlight comes as quite a shock.

These outdoor areas are where people gather for the 'entertainment.' Snake charmers, witch doctors, magicians and clowns are constantly performing, selling charms, herbs, fortunes. The snake charmers always have the largest audience. With cobra in basket and flute to lips, these men sway, trancelike, while the snake gradually emerges from its basket. With a series of symbolic gestures spiced with incantations, the charmer succeeds in coaxing the cobra out into the open. With shocked intakes of breath, the audience watches this spectacle, transfixed, breathing a collective sigh of relief when the snake slithers back into its nest and the basket lid closes, signifying the end of the show for the time being.

Another crowd pleaser is the majestic elephant. Even in Thailand where the sight of an elephant is much more common than in most other countries, the huge leathery beasts never fail to attract an audience. The elephant stands, swaying slightly, looking almost asleep. One foot is manacled to a nearby railing (a ridiculous precaution really, because if that elephant wanted to go, it would take a lot more than a railing to hold him). His trunk moves constantly, keeping flies away from his eyes and also sniffing out small treats that people offer him. His owner calls one and all to come ride the elephant. When he makes a sale, the elephant is made to bend down on his wrinkled front knees to allow the rider to mount - no easy task, even with the elephant kneeling.

As a study in contrasts, nearby is a small, almost-white goat, tethered to a metal stud hammered into the ground. He stands placidly chewing on the few bits of trodden-down grass he can find.

His owner, a large Thai lady with teeth blackened from many years of chewing betel nuts, sits nearby on an overturned wooden box, holding a huge circular basket that looks like a giant, upturned Frisbee. The basket is full of what looks like thick black tar, glinting in the sun. A closer look reveals thousands of black insects, looking suspiciously like cockroaches, but which are actually water bugs.

These creatures crawl under and over each other, creating a constantly moving mass. Even though the day is hot, the uninitiated experience a chill running down their spines at this sight. The fact that people actually eat these insects is mercifully unknown to the casual observer.

Cages filled with fluffy new chicks line the walls of many stores. These chickens have been dyed to make them more appealing to the customers, so there are hundreds of blue, orange and hot pink chicks that, despite their glamorous new coats, still say "Cheep, Cheep"!

Skinny boys and girls run barefoot through the crowds, holding up trinkets: bangles, hair barrettes, baby shoes, flower leis, Swiss Army knives, competing with each other to see who can get the highest price for their treasures. They know who to approach. There are tourists in abundance - pale-skinned, or glowing red from too much exposure to the sun, walking in a daze, staring open-mouthed at the assortment of sights.

They make easy marks, these farangs (foreigners). Their countries are undoubtedly richer than Thailand and, accordingly, goods are more expensive, so what would seem expensive to the residents sounds incredibly cheap to the visitors.

Young as they are, these children have picked up enough English, Japanese, French, and German to get by with just about any of the tourists. They bargain with serious faces, as though millions of dollars were involved in the transaction. Then, when their quarry has walked away examining their purchases, they roll their eyes in disbelief at their good fortune, running to tell as many friends as possible about the gullible farang who paid ten times what the item was worth without blinking an eye. Then they pound each other on the back, jumping up and down and laughing.

These children wear the simple costume of the street urchin - T-shirt and shorts. Some wear sandals, most wear nothing on their feet.

Older Thai males seem to wear long pants consistently, even though the temperature is over 100°F., often with almost 100% humidity.

Older Thai ladies wear the traditional, long sarong - the younger ones prefer Western clothing in all patterns and colors. Some of the combinations they come up with are startling: a bright purple tight skirt with a green, yellow and blue striped blouse, sprinkled with black spots for good measure; electric green, leg-hugging pants, together with a neon pink top with purple and red swirls. They're a colorful race of people, the Thai.

The people, the climate, the exotic foods and unusual animals all combine to make a trip to this special marketplace definitely worthwhile, for nowhere is there such a fascinating assortment as in the organized sprawl that is the Bangkok Weekend Market.